Edward Sylvester Ellis

Pontiac, chief of the Ottawas

A tale of the siege of Detroit

Edward Sylvester Ellis

Pontiac, chief of the Ottawas
A tale of the siege of Detroit

ISBN/EAN: 9783337174460

Printed in Europe, USA, Canada, Australia, Japan

Cover: Foto ©Andreas Hilbeck / pixelio.de

More available books at **www.hansebooks.com**

PONTIAC

CHIEF OF THE OTTAWAS

A TALE OF THE SIEGE OF DETROIT

BY

COLONEL H. R. GORDON

NEW YORK

E. P. DUTTON & COMPANY

31 WEST TWENTY-THIRD STREET

1897

CONTENTS.

ILLUSTRATIONS.

tispiece

PONTIAC,

CHIEF OF THE OTTAWAS.

CHAPTER I.

NIGHT ON THE RIVER.

CAPTAIN HORST, in charge of the small
schooner *Gladwyn* from Niagara, was as-
cending the Detroit river, on his way to the
frontier post of Detroit, which had been besieged
for several months by the great Pontiac, chief of the
Ottawas. It was the dream of that leader, as it had
been of King Philip, nearly a century before, to
unite all of his race against the whites and to wage
a remorseless war which should not end until the
last pale face was driven from the hunting grounds
of the red men.

The reader of American history hardly needs to be
reminded that at the conclusion of the French and
Indian war, France gave up by treaty all her domain
in the new world. Previous to the breaking out of
that war, she established a chain of military posts in

the west, her purpose being to found a great empire in the Mississippi valley. The capture of Quebec in 1759 foreshadowed so clearly the decisive end, that the famous ranger, Major Robert Rogers, was sent with an escort in the following year to receive the surrender of the French posts in the west. Detroit made its submission in November, in the presence of hundreds of Indians, who could not understand why so large a force of Frenchmen surrendered to so small a body of English soldiers.

But the sagacious Pontiac, who was among the spectators, grasped the whole meaning of the strange scene. "The Englishmen have conquered the French," he said, "and now they will turn on us and make us their slaves, but that shall never be."

And then the terrible leader of the Ottawas began forming that far-reaching conspiracy, which forms one of the most dramatic episodes in our history. The American Indian possesses in perfection the art of contenting his soul with patience, while awaiting the favorable moment for action. The weeks lengthened into months until full two years had come and gone, before the arrival of the day for striking the prodigious blow intended to wipe out every one of the English posts in the west.

Pontiac's messengers threaded their way through the dismal wilderness to tribes hundreds of miles distant, and in most cases secured their pledges to

join in the plot, which was as simple as it was com-
prehensive. It was, in short, that on May 7, 1763,
the Indians should attack the post nearest them and
then join in assailing the settlements. The plan was
successful in a number of instances, but Major Gladwyn, the commandant at Detroit, received warning
from an Ojibwa maiden and took such precautions
that when Pontiac and his warriors were admitted
within the palisades, under the pretense of making a
friendly call, they withdrew without firing a gun or
raising a hostile hand.

Pontiac kept up the semblance of friendship for
a short time, when, seeing that it was useless, he
threw aside all disguise and began the siege of Detroit. The tribes under his immediate control were
Ottawas, Ojibwas, Pottawatomies, and Wyandots,
afterward joined by others.

Detroit, at that time, was laid out in the form of
a square, inclosed by a high palisade. At each cor-
ner of this palisade was a wooden bastion, mounting
several pieces of artillery, and there were block-
houses over the gateway. The seventy-five or
eighty dwellings were separated by narrow streets
and were all made of wood. The garrison included
one hundred and twenty men, while a third as many
more were capable of bearing arms should the necessity arise. Two armed schooners lay near at hand
in the river.

This is not the place to give a detailed history of the siege of Detroit, which, beginning in May, had continued about three months, when the incidents we have set out to describe took place. In the interval, the Indians had tried without success to start a conflagration among the inflammable buildings of the post, and had failed to destroy by means of fire rafts, the schooners lying in the river. They had cut off supplies and reinforcements which tried to reach Detroit by way of the lake, and had inflicted a frightful defeat, with the loss of sixty killed and wounded, including the leader, Major Dalzell, in his attempt to surprise the besiegers.

Ever since that fateful day, the scene of the massacre has been known as Bloody Ridge, and it was during the following week that Captain Horst entered the river with his small sloop and crew of ten men, he being on his way with dispatches and provisions from Niagara for Major Gladwyn. The post had begun to feel the lack of supplies and could not hope to hold out much longer without help.

The captain's wish and expectation was to reach Detroit before night set in. The smart breeze carried the craft forward at a good rate, and the hopes of all were high, for every one comprehended the importance of reaching Detroit while daylight lasted. The wooded shores were the hiding-places of hundreds of scowling warriors, intently watching from cover the progress of the boat, but afraid to attack even with the smallness of the crew apparent, without the darkness to aid them. They were as anxious for the wind to die out as were the white men that it should hold, and sad to say the hopes of the warriors were gratified.

The breeze became fitful as the afternoon drew to a close, and each revival was fainter and weaker, until, just as twilight set in, the sails hung limp and the surface of the river became as smooth as a summer millpond.

Captain Horst had navigated the lakes and inland waters long enough to read unerringly all these signs. He knew there would not be another breath of air until the sun appeared above the horizon on the morrow.

" It 's no use," he said, compressing his lips and shaking his head, " we 're in for it, and are sure to see high jinks before we see Detroit."

" You 're right, Cap; the varmints are as thick as bees round a honeycomb, on both sides of the river."

" I have n't seen any."

" I hev," was the quiet response; " they don't show themselves if they can help it at such times as these, but I 've had more 'n one glimpse of 'em, consarn 'em !"

The *Gladwyn* was the smaller of the two schooners

which lay at Detroit during most of the siege, and which Pontiac had vainly attempted to destroy by means of fire rafts. It had been sent to Niagara with letters and dispatches, and was now returning with a crew of ten men, besides Horst, the master, and Jacobs, the mate. In addition there were six friendly Iroquois Indians, that had been allowed to go along as passengers.

When it was evident that the vessel could pass no further that night and the anchor was dropped, the Iroquois asked to be set ashore, saying they were in a hurry to reach their destination, which was not very definitely located. The master of the vessel did not like this request, and the veteran ranger, Jo Spain, shook his head.

" It means mischief," he said.

" You don't think they 'll join Pontiac ? "

" Not exactly, but it is n't sartin ; I 've had dealin's with the varmints before and they 're all alike. But they 're sure to make their way to Pontiac's camp and let him know how weak we are."

" Does n't he know that now ? "

" No ; how could he ? He has seen our men on deck, but he don't know that it is all of 'em ; he may think we 're keeping a lot out of sight, so as to give him and his warriors 'tickler thunder when they come out to tackle us."

" What shall I do, Jo ? "

The half-dozen Iroquois, wrapped in their blankets, despite the sultriness of the weather, were
standing sullenly apart near the bow, looking off to
the right in the direction of Fighting Island, opposite which the schooner was becalmed.

" You can't do anything but let 'em go."

The master of the craft showed his surprise at
this remark.

" You tell me to do the very thing I should n't
do."

" 'Cause you can't help it. It won't do to tie
these consarned varmints up, for some of 'em would
get loose during the fight, and then we shall have
them to fight, and that 'll be too much of a good
thing."

" Then it 's best to let them go, for if we refuse
and don't bind them, they will take the chance to
slip overboard, and in revenge will join our enemies."

The ranger nodded his head.

" You 've hit the idee 'zactly. I 'm powerful
sorry that they want to leave us just at this time;
when I heerd 'em talkin' it over among themselves,
I tried to argufy 'em out of it, but when an Injin
has sot his mind on anything, you may as well give
up, so I told 'em we 'd set 'em ashore."

" What did they say to that ? "

" Grunted and nodded their heads. Red Feather,

the leader, said he and the rest was our friends, and if there was any trouble, they 'd come back and fight for us. I tried to make 'em b'leve I swallered that, but it was hard work.''

'' Shall we take them ashore in the boat or let them swim ? ''

'' It would n't do to make 'em swim, for that would hurt their feelin's. They 'd know why we done it, and it would give 'em an excuse for helpin' Pontiac.''

'' Do they need an excuse ? ''

'' Mebbe, I 'm wrong,'' said Jo, after a moment's reflection, during which he glanced at the dusky figures near the prow, rapidly growing indistinct in the gathering gloom; '' I may be mistook, but I hev a hope that Red Feather and the rest won't do anything more 'n to tell Pontiac that there 's only a dozen of us.''

'' What is your reason for hoping that ? ''

'' These Iroquois, you know, stood by us purty well in the war that 's about come to an end; them six tribes that make up the Iroquois people are strong enough to clean out all the other varmints in the country. Consequently and aforesaid, they would do as they danged please. Pontiac would be tickled to death if he could get the Iroquois to jine him in this bus'ness, but they 've got too much sense. When these half a dozen go into his camp

he darsen't try to make 'em do what they don't
want to do, 'cause he knows the Iroquois at home
would n't stand it. When they larned of it they 'd
clean out all the Ottawas, Ojibwas, Pottawatomies,
and Wyandots in the country. That 's the kind
of folks the Iroquois are. But all the same, these
varmints nat'rally wish Pontiac well, and they 'll let
'em know how many men we have aboard. Pontiac
will feel mighty good over it. He 's been tryin' to
burn this schooner, and now he 'll know of a sar-
tinty that the Great Spirit has give it into his
hands.''

" You speak as if Pontiac is with the Indians
along shore. We are nine miles below Detroit: is
it not more probable that he is near the fort ? ''

" Wal, as to that, there 's no sayin'. Mebbe he
is n't on the bank over to the left or on Fightin'
Island, off there to the right. I don't know that it
makes much difference one way or t'other. We 're
bound to catch it sure to-night.''

" It will be a risky thing to take these Iroquois
ashore.''

" I 'll take 'em,'' remarked Jo, as he might have
remarked that he would eat his dinner when it was
ready; " it 's 'bout dark 'nough.''

The ranger sauntered to the bow of the schooner,
where the six dusky passengers stood apart from the
crew, talking together now and then in low tones.

Jo Spain had the peculiar gift of readily learning an Indian tongue, and he could talk to these warriors as well as to his own people. Not only that, but he was familiar with the Ottawa and several other Indian lingoes.

The Iroquois held their heads bent, their coarse black hair dangling about their shoulders, and they glanced sideways at the white man as he drew near. They formed a picturesque group, with their stained feathers in the crowns of their heads, but they seemed to feel some pleasure at the approach of the famous fighter of their race.

".Does my brothers wish to go ashore?" he asked, addressing himself more directly to Red Feather, who replied:

" It is our wish, but the Iroquois are the brothers of the English."

" You have showed that more 'n once," was the diplomatic comment of Jo; " it shall be as you wish; we 'll step into the boat, and I 'll take you to land. Come with me."

CHAPTER II.

THE ranger walked to the stern of the schooner, where the small boat was fastened. Captain Horst saluted the Indians as they passed, and bade them good-by. They grunted in reply, and stepped carefully into the boat, which they would have liked better had it been a canoe, to which they were accustomed, but they showed no hesitation, for the craft was capable of carrying a greater number than they. They had seen such row-boats before, and they took their seats with judgment.

Jo was the last one to enter, unfastening the rope before he did so. Then, instead of using the two oars, as is the custom, he employed one as a paddle, following the fashion of the Indians, by dipping it first on one side of the boat and then on the other. He was seated at the stern, and by adopting this method he faced all of his undesirable passengers.

There could be no question as to the extreme danger of the task the ranger had undertaken. He was not only in the power of these six Iroquois, every one of whom carried a rifle and knife, but he was approaching land where there was no doubt of the intense hostility of the savages lurking along the bank. It was questionable whether Red Feather and his companions could save him from harm if the Ottawas offered it, and equally questionable whether they would do so if the opportunity was theirs.

To the astonishment of Captain Horst, Jo left his rifle behind him upon enterng the smaller boat. But there was reason in his action, because if danger should come the single weapon could not save him, and he would be handicapped by the necessity of taking care of it. If anything would appeal to the chivalry of the Iroquois (admitting that any of the people possessed that virtue) this apparent trust in their honor would do so.

In leaving the *Gladwyn*, Jo Spain headed toward Fighting Island, on his right, but was hardly out of sight of the schooner when Red Feather told him that it was their desire to land upon the mainland, to the left.

" It shall be as my brother wishes," replied the ranger, immediately turning the boat about, taking care, however, to pass the schooner at such a distance that it could not be seen.

The critical question with Jo was whether there was any understanding between the Iroquois in his small boat and the Ottawas on the mainland. If such were the fact, he knew his fate was sealed, but with all his acuteness and suspicion, he could not believe that anything of the kind existed. The schooner had been continually moving until the failure of the wind at nightfall, and no communication could have passed between the parties during that time.

It was impossible that an agreement was made before the vessel left Fort Niagara, for no one could have foreseen the present situation of affairs. On the whole, therefore, the ranger believed that the only peril to which he was likely to be exposed was that which developed with the progress of incidents themselves.

He carefully plied the oar, and in due time the faint outline of the towering trees showed that he was near shore. He held his course at right angles until the branches were almost over his head, when, by a dextrous flirt of the paddle, he shot the boat fully fifty feet further up stream.

" Why does my brother do that ? " angrily asked Red Feather, turning his scowling face toward him.

" The place is not good for my brother's feet," was the calm reply, though Jo was influenced by a far different reason.

" All places are good for the feet of the Iroquois."

" Very well, then, we 'll land here."

And as he spoke the words, he drove the bow of

the craft so hard against the bank that it stopped with a bump so sudden that every one was jarred.

It was a trying moment, and the ranger was listening for some signal or the rush of the Ottawas. The Iroquois rose slowly and left the boat. Jo bade them good-by again, and, hardly able to repress his anxiety, instantly pushed out from shore, plying the oar with the utmost vigor at his command.

And this was the most trying moment of all. The sharp question of Red Feather was a betrayal of his feelings, and Jo half expected that the whole six would let fly at him, with the intervening space so brief that a miss was impossible. His position was much like that of an officer trying to preserve his dignity while walking away from an enemy aiming at him. In fact, when sure that the impetus of the boat would take it beyond sight, Jo dropped down in the bottom, where he was protected from any bullets that might whistle about his ears.

But not a shot was fired, a fact which led him to conclude that Red Feather and his companions were indifferent as to what befell him and the rest.

" They don't care about my scalp, but they 'll let the other varmints know there 's only a dozen of us to defend the schooner, and maybe the Iroquois will help in the attack, so as to keep their hands in."

When about to resume the paddle, he heard a

gentle plash in the water. All sounds were significant at such times, and he suspected that an enemy
was swimming toward him. His keen sense of hearing told him precisely the point whence came the
noise, and he cautiously peered over the side of the
boat, hoping to catch sight of his foe.

" One thing 's sartin," thought the ranger, " if
he 's got his gun with him he can't use it in the
water—so we stand the same as to that."

Jo Spain did not carry a pistol, for that weapon
of those days was a clumsy and unhandy affair.
The rangers depended upon their unerring rifles and
upon their knives when it came to a hand-to-hand
encounter.

He failed to detect anything suspicious, and, imprudent though it might seem, he settled into the
belief that the slight disturbance was caused by a
fish, which, as they are fond of doing on still summer nights, had flung itself in sport out of the
water.

Still, the keen eyes of the ranger continually
roamed over the water on every side, as he swung
the paddle. He had calculated the distance so
accurately that he was not obliged to swerve to the
right or left, after catching sight of the motionless
schooner.

" Is that you, Jo ?" called Captain Horst, in a
guarded undertone.

" It 's me," was the reply, as the ranger ran the little boat under the stern of the larger craft, climbed out and made it fast.

" I 'm greatly relieved to see you back," said the master, " for it was a risky venture to make, but you came from the direction of the mainland."

" After heading fur the island, Red Feather told me he wanted to land on t'other shore, so I took 'em there. We had n't any fuss in partin'. What 's to be the end I don't know, but I 'm glad we 're rid of 'em."

Captain Horst had lost no time in making ready for the attack of their enemies. Many of the preparations were made immediately after dropping the anchor, so as to impress the Indians with their watchfulness. The single small cannon on board was loaded to the muzzle with slugs and scrap iron and would be a most effective weapon at short range. Every man of the twelve owned a rifle. In truth, there were three or four extra ones. Ammunition was plentiful, most of the men possessed knives, and there were several hatchets and axes. It was certain that the assailants would receive a fierce reception whenever they came.

Everything that could be done had been done when Jo Spain walked to the stern of the schooner with the captain, where they could converse a little apart from the rest.

" It can't do any good to speculate as to what Red Feather and the others will do, and I don't think six makes much difference where there 's so many. I wonder that they did n't open fire on us from the shore when we were in such plain sight, after the wind died out and I had to drop anchor. But they did not even show themselves, though they could have picked off some of us."

" Thar 's nuthin' that a redskin likes so much as to 'sprise an enemy; them varmints don't want us to think they 've any idee of botherin' us; they mean to come out here to-night, and hope we won't be 'spectin' anything of the kind. If one of 'em had let fly at us, it would have upset their whole plan. You catch the idee, Cap ? "

The bronzed captain nodded his head, holding his thin lips compressed, while his gray eyes glittered. He had been an active partisan in the French and Indian war, barely closed, and few understood the treacherous nature of the redmen better than he. He required no argument to convince him that he would never see Detroit without a desperate fight with the followers of Pontiac, who had been told by the French settlers that the king of their country was asleep, but would soon awake and come to help them drive all the English from the country.

It was noticeable that the crew of the schooner, in making their dispositions for the night, almost involuntarily, as may be said, protected themselves, so far as they could, while moving about the craft. As there was no telling from which shore the blow would come, the slender masts were of little avail, but the furtive glance, the haste from one point to another, the ducking of the head, and the numerous evidences of misgiving were so common that the captain reproved the brave fellows more than once, setting the example by standing as erect as if his boat were in the middle of Lake Erie.

"When do you suppose they will attack us?" was the captain's question.

The ranger shook his head.

"The fav'rite time with the varmints is just afore daylight, when white folks sleep the soundest, but they don't always wait that long.   It depends on sarcumstances; they 'll wait till they think we 've give up the idea of their comin', and then they 'll be down on us like a house afire."

"We must not let them come over the rail," said Captain Horst, with another flash of his fine gray eyes.

"No, sir; fur, if you do, we 're gone!   They will attack in such a swarm that they won't need mor'n half a chance; if they get that, it will be good-by to us all; they 'll scoop every scalp in the crowd."

"When I find hope gone, I 'll blow up the boat!

If we have got to go to kingdom come, we 'll send more of 'em in the other direction.''

There was no braggadocio in these words. The master would not hesitate to carry out his resolution.

'' That hits me right,'' remarked the ranger, as if communing with himself, as his restless eyes roved from shore to shore; '' when you find you 've got to go, why do it in style ! As I take it, there 's 'nough powder aboard to blow this old vessel sky high.''

'' Yes; we have several hundred pounds, intended for Major Gladwyn; it will be a good deal better to go out with that than to have the Indians finish us, by tomahawk or stake.''

'' Of course, not forgetting that it will make a purty good-sized hole in Pontiac's people at the same time—but, here 's Asher, who looks as if he wanted to say something.''

The faces of the two veterans lit up, as a young man, not more than eighteen years of age, came toward them, making a half-military salute to both as if apologizing for his intrusion. He saw he was welcome, for he was a favorite with the crew of the sloop, and with none to a greater degree than to the captain and the old ranger.

Asher Norris was the nephew of Jo Spain, and his father, mother, and most intimate friends were in

Detroit. He had left that post some months before with his uncle, and made the long journey to Niagara bearing an urgent request from Major Gladwyn for supplies. The result of the trip was the attempt of the schooner to deliver the much-needed stores, which, when almost at the gate of the post, were placed in a position of the gravest peril.

CHAPTER III.

THROUGH THE SHADOWS.

"WHAT a pity that the breeze did not last an hour or two longer," said young Asher Norris, with a sigh; "we are only eight or nine miles from Detroit, and a little more wind would have taken us there."

"There 's no use in crying for spilt milk," was the philosophic remark of Captain Horst. "Jo and I, and, I suppose, you, too, have made up our minds that we 're to have the sharpest kind of a fight to-night."

"I was sure of that as soon as the anchor was dropped. But," added Asher, touching the matter that had brought him to the stern of the schooner, and that wrinkled the brow of his handsome face, "why can't we lower the boat that Uncle Jo just used, and with all of us that can get into it, tow the vessel out of this dangerous spot?"

The ranger shook his head.

"'T won't never do."

"I had thought of the same thing," remarked the skipper; "it would be hard work, but we might get the schooner to the fort by daylight."

Jo shook his head more decisively than before.

" What would be the end ?   Both shores is lined with the varmints; they can see like owls in the night, and when they ain't able to see they can hear a leaf as it falls from the tree. No matter how carefully we might handle the oars, they 'd catch the first stroke we made; they 'd know what it meant ; they 'd be out in the stream by the hundred and cut us off from the sloop by gettin' themselves between; then we 'd be in a purty scrape, would n't we ? If we should do just what the varmints want, it would be the very thing aforesaid which my young nephew has proposed, meaning no harm but good to all consarned."

The ranger looked meaningly at the youth, who flushed at the good-natured but hardly the less cutting reproof. There was so much sense in the words of the veteran that neither Asher nor Captain Horst presumed to argue the question.

" Then I suppose," added the young man, after a moment's silence, " that the only thing we can do is to lie low and wait for them to attack us."

" You hit it that time square, but I 've been thinkin' that after all there is a little bit more we can do—that is, mebbe."

His friends looked inquiringly at him.

" From the signs I observed to-day the redskins are on both sides of the river, but I 've an idee that a good deal the most of 'em are over there on the left on the mainland. Bime by I 'll swim ashore and take a look 'round.''

'' It will be very risky, and what good will you accomplish ? ''

'' When you an' me was fightin' under Colonel Washington, Cap, you remember he allers tried to find out what the French was goin' to do. When he larned that he knowed how to get ready for 'em. If I can find out how many of Pontiac's varmints are in the woods, and can hear some of 'em talkin', why I may pick up a little vallyble information.''

Captain Horst could not look upon the proposal as did he who offered it. He felt the need of every one to repel the attack that was sure to be made within a few hours, and the absence of Jo Spain would be as serious as that of two or three of his best men. And yet he was backward about opposing this veteran of the woods. He held his peace.

As if reading his thoughts, Jo said:

'' I don't intend to desart you, Cap, and mean to be back here afore the first gun is fired or the first yawp made.''

'' I have no doubt that such is your intention, Jo,'' was the significant response.

'' And I 'll do it, too.''

This was uttered with an emphasis that lifted a

weight of apprehension from the shoulders of
the captain, as well as from those of Asher
Norris.

" And yet if you go to the left bank you will
leave the island unvisited, and the real danger, after
all, may be from that side."

" I 'll visit both."

" Before you return ? "

The ranger was silent a minute, as if this phase of
the question had not presented itself to him.

" No; I 'll go to the left bank of the stream, larn
what is to be larned, swim back to the sloop and
then swim across to t' other bank, lettin' you know,
of course, what I 've larned on my first visit.
P'raps I may run agin Red Feather once more."

Asher Norris had nothing to add. He was a
young man, less given to talk than his relative, but
had one who knew his nature studied him at this
moment, he would have come to the belief that the
words of the ranger had turned his thoughts in a
new direction, and he was forming some plan of his
own—one that he did not deem it best to explain
to the others.

Though there was a partial moon overhead, the
sultry sky was so overspread with clouds that not a
twinkling star was visible. Occasionally a few faint
rays stole through the ragged edges of vapor, but
the light was so weak that it was hardly visible, and

served rather to make the darkness more profound and all-pervading.

While the three were conversing in low tones, and the others were gathered here and there about the deck, speaking in whispers, listening, and with all their senses on the alert, the little schooner lay as if becalmed in the middle of the Atlantic.

The stillness was profound. From the direction of Detroit came the faint report of a gun, sounding many miles away. It was probably fired by one of the sentinels at some redskin whom he discovered prowling around the palisades, and which was sufficient to drive off the skulker, since the shot was not repeated. Then was heard the bark of a fox, and the long-drawn, dismal howl of a wolf echoed from somewhere down the river. Were he and his companions growing impatient over the delayed feast, and were they slinking from the gloomy recesses and licking their chops in anticipation of what was coming?

Having decided upon his course of action, Jo Spain did not wait a minute beyond the time he thought necessary. He was attired in the usual hunting shirt and leggings worn by the men who spent most of their lives in the woods a hundred years ago. History has related many of the exploits of Major Rogers and his famous rangers, and among them all was none braver and more skilled in woodcraft than this man, a native of New Hampshire, who served with the daring leader down to the day when the surrender of Detroit took place.

Jo fastened his long flint-lock rifle to his shoulder, muzzle downward, so that the stock protruded above his shoulders and the crown of his head. Thus, if he had only plain swimming to do and was not compelled to sink below the surface, he would be able to save the charge of his gun from becoming wet. If, however, he should be forced to dive, the charge would have to be withdrawn and a new one rammed home.

" Wal, I 'm off," he quietly observed, when the weapon was tied in place.

" Good luck to you ! " said the captain in a low voice.

The ranger climbed over the gunwale at the stern, where it was not far above the water, and making use of the rudder, upon which he rested his large, mocassin-covered foot, silently let himself down into the Detroit river. The current was not strong, and in the sultry hush of the summer night the cool embrace of the water was refreshing and grateful.

Captain Horst and Asher Norris had stepped to the stern and were peering down at the veteran. In the gloom they could see his sinewy figure, as he set himself free from the schooner, with no more noise than that made by the gentle rippling at the

prow of the craft. They saw, too, the head covered
with the coon-skin cap, but only for a moment,
when it vanished and all was as it had been before.

"Confound it!" muttered the captain, "I'm
sorry he has left; I don't believe it will do any
good, and he's running into the worst sort of
danger."

"But he has done the same thing many times
before."

"And is just the man to do it once too often.
He has had such good luck in the past that he
thinks it'll stick by him to the end, when puff! one
of these days he'll be wiped out by some Indian
boy of no more than half your years."

"I don't think so," was the quiet reply of Asher
Norris; "at first his proposition did not strike me
favorably, but I now believe he did a wise thing."

"Well, we shall speedily know, for business will
be humming pretty soon."

Meanwhile, Jo Spain was making the best of his
opportunity. He was swimming slowly, silently,
and with the utmost care. His eyes being so near
the surface of the water, he was at considerable
advantage in that respect. His naturally sharp
vision allowed nothing to escape him which it would
have been possible for any one to see.

He was unquestionably right when he declared
that the Indians lurking on the shore of the river

would wait until there was reason to believe the crew of the sloop were partly, if not wholly, disarmed of suspicion.   A surprise is the favorite method of attack with the redmen.

Having shaken himself clear of the schooner, Jo swam toward Detroit, still holding his place near the middle of the stream.   If the hostiles were looking for some such reconnoissance, they would expect the man making it to approach the shore on either side when seeking to land.   Therefore, the ranger did not draw near the left bank until more than a hundred yards from the schooner.

Even at that point, the Indians might be on the watch, and no approach could have been more guarded.   Jo swam low in the water, aware that in spite of it the projecting rifle stock would tell the fatal story, if he happened to draw near to some dusky sentinel.   Accordingly, he held himself ready to drop below the surface on the first appearance of anything suspicious.

The bank was lined with trees and a species of undergrowth which dipped over the current and offered the best possible hiding-place for an enemy.

Neither eye nor ear could detect anything amiss, and the white man had already increased his rate of progress, having fixed in his mind the point where he would emerge, when he caught the ripple as if made by some person stepping stealthily into the stream. On the instant and without the slightest noise, Jo sank out of sight, just as if some monster of the deep had seized his foot and drawn him under.

The water was not deep so near shore, so that while he was still descending his moccasins touched the soft bottom. He held the points of the compass in mind, and, without coming up to the air, swam swiftly inward. He had planned where he would emerge, and hit it to a hair.

Instead of rising from the surface some feet from shore, he did so close to the bank, and directly under the overhanging vegetation, thus shutting himself from the sight of any suspicious eye that might be peering out upon the stream. The danger was that the slight but unavoidable rustling thus created would be heard by an enemy; but, since there was peril everywhere, no matter what he did, the ranger did not hesitate.

Resting a minute with his head and shoulders above the current, he listened, but heard nothing to cause alarm. His vision could be of no help in his situation, and he did not count upon it. A second or two later, he had entirely emerged from the river, and was seated in his dripping garments on the bank, still listening and as vigilant as ever.

" It could n't have been one of the varmints, after all," he muttered, alluding to the rippling which sent him toward the bottom; "I might as well have stayed whar I was, and come out of the river without ruinin' the powder in old Bess, but, as the captain obsarved, thar 's no use of cryin' fur spilt milk. The varmints must be somewhar not very fur off, and I don't go back to the vessel till I larn something as is worth larnin', fur I feel it in my bones that ugly times are powerful clus."

It was the rule with men of his profession not to stir from a spot after firing a gun, until it was reloaded, so as to have it ready for instant use, but Jo Spain decided to break that wholesome rule in the present instance.

CHAPTER IV.

THE LEFT SHORE.

JO SPAIN refrained from drawing the charge from his rifle and ramming home a new one, through fear of betraying his presence to some of his enemies, who, he was satisfied, were in his immediate neighborhood. It was no easy task to unload and load one of the old-fashioned flint-lock weapons in profound darkness, though he had done it, and the necessity was not urgent.

The course of the ranger was now down stream, toward the schooner, as he supposed the main body of hostiles would be found in that direction. That he had placed himself in an exceedingly " ticklish " position was manifest the next moment, when he caught a faint, bird-like whistle, a short distance ahead and to one side, which he knew was made by a warrior stealing through the forest; but if this discovery was startling, that which immediately followed was more so. The reply, almost instantly made, was of the same character, and came from a point so directly close and behind him that he fairly caught his breath, believing he had been discovered.

But such was not the fact. In the deep vegetation of the woods and with the new moon veiled by dense clouds, the darkness was absolutely impenetrable. He could see no one and no one could see him. He was in a crouching posture, feeling each inch of the way. His hand had touched the shaggy bark of a tree and he now straightened up, as near as possible to the trunk, where he was less likely to be bumped against by a dusky scout than if standing alone.

That matters were becoming extraordinarily critical was proved the next instant, when, with his sense of hearing trained to an incredibly fine point, he distinctly heard his enemy on the other side of the tree. Not only that, but his hand touched the rough covering, and he, too, straightened up. Thus the white and red man stood, with only the thickness of a tree trunk separating them. One was aware of the presence of the other, and the white man began to doubt as to the knowledge of the other regarding himself.

He laid his hand on his knife, which was not fastened at his waist or hip, but over the left breast, where it could be seized more handily than from any other place. If the warrior groped around the tree, he must of necessity come in collision with the other, though Jo lessened the chance by taking a single step backward. The advantage was with the ranger, for he would know precisely where to strike the instant the other touched him, while it began to look as if the red man did not suspect the presence of the other, for, with such knowledge, he would not have dared to reply so promptly to the call of his comrade. This was shown at the end of another minute, when, instead of waiting for a second signal, he himself repeated it, and was answered from a point a few rods away.

The situation of Jo Spain was not made any more comfortable by the discovery that the Indian, almost within arm's reach, instead of going to his companion, was waiting for the latter to come to him. Inasmuch as this would have made the situation altogether too perilous, Jo took two more backward steps. He did so with amazing skill, and yet with the almost inaudible rustling of a twig caught the attention of the keen-eared warrior in his front.

But there might have been any one of half a dozen causes to explain the slight noise, without the right one being suspected, and the warrior seemed to give it no further thought. Almost immediately he was joined by the other, and the two began conversing in their gruff, guttural fashion.

Jo Spain was delighted to discover that, instead of using Iroquois, they spoke in the Ottawa tongue. He was almost as familiar with that as with his own.

3

Naturally their voices were low, but they were so near that in the utter silence not a syllable escaped the eavesdropper. The very opportunity he was seeking had come to him. He expected to grope for perhaps an hour through the wood with slight chance of success, but he had hardly touched foot upon land when success met him.

A liberal translation of the conversation might be as follows :

" My brother comes from the other shore of the river; where is the mighty Pontiac ? Is he with his warriors ?"

" He is with his warriors, and there are many brave Ojibwas with him."

" He has seen the canoe of the white man, the great canoe which floats through the water when the wind blows."

" Pontiac has seen the big canoe; he has watched it as it came up the river; he knew the Great Spirit would give it into his hand, as he will all the white people when our father wakes from his sleep on the other side of the great water and drives the English from the hunting grounds of the redmen."

" There are many warriors on this side of the river, and they will go with Pontiac when his canoes come out from the shore to slay the big canoe of the white men."

" But the warriors on this side are not so many as

on the island. When the moon is off there then we will slay the big canoe of the white men."

Even so experienced a ranger as Jo Spain was puzzled to understand the full meaning of this last remark. The night was impenetrable, and how one of the warriors could make clear to the other the future location of the orb during that night was impossible to explain, unless he took hold of his companion's hand and indicated it by the sense of feeling.

As it was the ranger could gain no idea of the hour fixed for the attack upon the sloop, and the knowledge of such date was not important. It was liable to change by Pontiac, who often showed a whimsicality of motive. It was enough to know that the fierce assault was certain to be made by parties of Indians coming from both sides of the river, and moving as nearly as possible at the same moment. It remained for Captain Horst and his crew to be on the alert until the danger should come and go. It was noticeable, too, that these Ottawas made no reference to the Iroquois that had been landed on their side of the river.

" Will the white men know of our coming ? " was the query of the Ottawa who had last reached the tree.

" No," replied his companion; " their eyes have been closed. They know not that the woods are full of brave Ottawas and Ojibwas; they will lie down to sleep, with only one left to keep his eyes open, and he, too, will fall into slumber."

" And just there," reflected the listening white man, " is where you are making a mistake, my copper-colored friend."

The scout would have chuckled over the fact but for the terrible dread that, even if alert, the defenders of the sloop were too few to repel the overwhelming assault of the Ottawas and Ojibwas. The reflection caused an intense, almost irrestrainable hatred to flame up in his heart. It was intolerable to hear these two miscreants exulting over the prospect of massacring every person on board the becalmed vessel, a short distance away. Jo's rifle was still fastened behind his shoulders, so as to leave free play for his arms, and his iron-like fingers closed around the handle of his knife, as he bent forward to catch a few more words.

" The white men may have seen Pontiac and his warriors," ventured the one that had evidently spent most of his time on this side of the stream.

" They have seen none of them," was the reassuring response of the other, " for did not Pontiac declare he would slay all who showed themselves to the white men ?"

" I wish he 'd do it," grimly reflected the eavesdropper, " for I seed nigh onto twenty, and there would be that many less to fight."

" Then we shall wait till the signal comes from Pontiac."

The Ottawas abruptly ceased talking, and several minutes of silence followed, while Jo Spain listened for further information.

Then it occurred to him that there was nothing more to learn. He had found out of a verity that a large force intended to attack the schooner in overwhelming numbers, at an hour that night, when they believed the defenders would be off their guard. The warriors would come from both sides of the river, and it was not impossible from up and down stream, with a view of making the assault resistless.

There seemed to be no call for staying longer, especially as the scout meant to reconnoitre the other shore before taking his place on the sloop to await the crisis; but his anger against these two redmen rose to a white heat.

" It 's my Christian dooty to make their numbers as few as I can," he thought, as he drew his formidable knife from its sheath, " and, by heavens, I 'll do it ! "

He was not the one to hesitate when forming such a resolution. The sound of the voices had located the two Ottawas, and he felt sure of striking them, as sure, indeed, as if the sun were shining.

The powerful right arm was drawn back, he

crouched low, and making a quick, light leap, brought down his hand with all the vicious fierceness at his command. It would have been a relief had he dared to emit a triumphant yell at that instant, but discretion restrained.

The terrible weapon, however, swished through vacancy; the Ottawas had departed. He was not the only one that could move in absolute silence through the woods at night.

"That 's the time Jo Spain made a fool of himself!" he muttered; "I 'm glad no one seed me, and I 'll hev to be powerful short of things to talk about with my friends for me to introdooce the same as a subject for remarks."

He decided not to enter the river where he had left it, but considerably farther down stream. This would bring him nearly opposite the schooner, though it was impossible for him exactly to locate it, since it was invisible and not so much as a point of light was shown on the vessel.

Jo did not need the knowledge that the woods were full of redmen to make him guarded in every movement. He was but a short distance from the river, but it was a long time before his wet moccasins again touched its brink. He noticed that the undergrowth was less abundant, and, in spite of his care, he came within a hair of stepping into a large canoe drawn up against the bank. Had there been any one in it, he must assuredly have detected the approach of a stranger.

The ranger groped about to learn whether there were any others near, but in the limited space examined he found none.

" There 's one thing mighty sartin," he thought, " when these varmints come to get into their blamed canoes, they 'll find one of 'em is n't of much account."

With the aid of his knife he cut several gaping seams in the frail structure. The gurgling water told that the craft was likely to disappoint the parties who intended to make their voyage to the schooner in it. Even in committing this act of mischief, Jo paused long enough to consider its prudence. But, so far as he saw, there was no way in which it could recoil upon him. The Indians were not likely to suspect that it had been done by a white man, and even if they did, it would lessen their confidence in their own ability to destroy their intended victims. Had there been any other canoes within easy reach, he would have slitted them in the same ruthless style.

With the utmost caution he made his way into the river until the water reached his shoulders, when he sank lower, and began swimming in the direction, as he believed, of the schooner; but so long as the outlines of the shore could be discerned in the gloom, he gave more attention to the rear than to the front. There was no evidence that his presence had been detected by his enemies, and he soon swam with more freedom and with his eyes to the front.

Near the middle of the stream, and when confident he was close to his friends, he failed to see anything of the craft, with its familiar single masts and short dark hull. With all his woodcraft and a certain remarkable skill in keeping his bearings in the absence of landmarks, he had lost the boat.

" But it can't be far off," he thought, after making sure that he had swam far enough out in the stream; " it 's either farther up or farther down, and I must find it after awhile."

Fifteen minutes later, he checked himself, and supplemented his conclusion by the proviso, " I don't know whether I will or not; either the confounded vessel or me is lost, and I don't know which it is."

Facing about, he swam vigorously in the opposite course, feeling that he was losing valuable time, for it remained his intention to make a visit to Fighting Island before the attack from the Indians, which might take place earlier than he had first supposed.

CHAPTER V.

THE RIGHT SHORE.

CAPTAIN HORST waited for several minutes at the stern of his schooner after the ranger had swam away and vanished in the night. Then he walked forward and talked in low tones with his men. He found them determined and fully alive to the perils that impended.

"Surrender, boys, you know, is not to be thought of, for no mercy is to be expected from Pontiac or any of his warriors."

"Nor from any redman," growled a stalwart boatman from New York; "did n't I fall into their hands three years ago, near Niagara? And did n't they tie me to a tree and start the fire about me, when a French officer dashed the wood aside and gave me a chance to run for my life? I think I know the breed."

"That 's precisely the way they served Israel Putnam when he was out with Rogers' rangers, and he was saved in the same way."

"You don't need to tell us not to think of surrender, Cap," said Mate Jacobs; "all the same, it looks to me as if they 'll be too many for us. What 's to be done when that minute comes ? ''

'' You 've got the magazine ready ? ''

'' Yes, sir.''

'' When I sing out to you, ' Blow her up ! ' why, touch her off.''

'' I 'll do it as sure as my name is Jack Carson,'' was the response.

'' Very well; we understand each other,'' and the captain walked back to the stern, where Asher Norris was standing near the cabin.

'' What 's the meaning of that ? ''

The question of Captain Horst was asked as he stepped close to his young friend and noticed that he had fastened his rifle to his back, precisely as Jo Spain did before leaving the vessel.

'' I 'm going ashore,'' was the quiet response.

'' You forget that Jo has already done that.''

'' No; he has taken the left shore; I 'm going to Fighting Island.''

'' But I do not commend the plan,'' said the captain, gravely; '' that will leave only ten, and we need double the number.''

'' He expects to be back before an attack is made, and I am just as confident as he that I shall be with you.''

'' His intention is to find out how matters stand on one shore, to report, and then to do the same on the island. He can do it more effectually than you, for he has ten times the experience."

"It would be presumptuous in me to dispute with you, Captain, but Jo may be kept so long on one side of the river that he will not have time to examine the other. While he is busy on his ground, I will be at work on mine."

Despite the plausible argument of the young man, the captain was far from being convinced. Had Asher Norris been a member of his crew he would not have permitted the venture. But Asher and his uncle were really only a couple of passengers, who had come on the schooner at Niagara. He was glad to have their company, for they were valuable men, but from the first they had done as they chose, without looking to him for orders.

The only one who was in a position to command the youth was absent. Had he been present it is safe to say the risk never would have been taken by the nephew. As it was, no one could say him nay.

"Well, act as you please, Asher, but in my judgment you are doing a thing not only unnecessary, but dangerous."

"Perhaps you are right," replied the youth, impressed by the gravity of his senior, "but we will leave that to the future."

And then, bidding the captain good-night, he imitated the action of his relative, climbing over the bow, stepping on the rudder, and letting himself softly down into the water. A minute later he, too, disappeared in the darkness, and the captain looked off in the gloom, much oppressed by what had taken place.

" That leaves ten of us," he remarked to Mate Jacobs, who, overhearing the conversation, had joined him; " as likely as not, we shall never see either of them again."

" It 's all tomfoolery," said the mate, more impatient than the master; " we 've made up our mind that we 're bound to have a visit from the Indians, and that 's all we need to know. It is n't likely that Pontiac or any of his imps will be kind enough to tell Jo or his nephew the exact minute when we 're to expect them. I know that Jo had some good reason to leave, and he wants to help us, but I 've a suspicion of that cub."

" And what is it ? "

" That he means to sneak through the woods to Detroit; so long as he can save his own hide, why need he care for us ? "

But the captain would not accept that view.

" I am sure it is nothing of that sort. Asher is one of the bravest young men I ever met. When we ran into shore to get some firewood, along the lake, some days ago, have you forgotten how he helped cover the retreat of you and Jameson ? "

" I 'll give him credit for that; he 's full of pluck, but some men show the same thing, when danger comes upon them sudden like. He may have been thinking the thing over, and made up his mind that the best thing he could do is to light out."

" If you live long enough to get out of this scrape, you 'll admit you did the young man an injustice."

" I hope so, but since he has gone, why can't we all do the same ? "

The question surprised the captain.

" You mean for each of us to steal away from the fort, swim as far up the stream as we can and thus circumvent Pontiac ? "

" That 's it; what 's to hinder ? "

The captian was inclined at first to think well of the plan, strangely as it struck him. A brief thought, however, settled the matter.

" I 'll never desert the schooner as long as I 'm able to defend her. We must stand by her to the last. We set out to furnish Major Gladwyn with powder, and we 've enough on board to serve him several months. Now, to hand over that powder to Pontiac will be like joining him to help take Detroit."

" That 's a view I did n't think of, and there 's truth in it, but we could pitch the powder into the river."

" It 's not to be thought of," remarked the cap-

tain, in a quiet but so determined a voice that no
more persuasion was attempted.   All gave their
attention to watching, listening, and waiting for the
trial that must soon come.

Meanwhile, Asher Norris, young, active, and lusty,
swam with silent and powerful strokes toward the
shore of the island, invisible in the gloom, but whose
direction was easily kept in mind, by the flow of the
current.   When the dim outlines of the wooded
bank took form in the gloom, he slackened his speed
and allowed himself to drift farther down stream
before making a landing.   Finally, when, so far as
he could judge, the way was clear, he propelled
himself forward with several swift strokes until his
feet touched bottom, and then stepped out among
the limbs and undergrowth, and crouched in the
darkness.

There was little difference between the two shores,
so far as appearances went, both being thickly
wooded.   He could hear nothing, but, hoping to
make some valuable discovery, he threaded his way
among the trees, taking a course at right angles to
the stream until he had penetrated a distance of
fully a hundred yards.   Then, as he was beginning
to ask himself whether the whole attack would not
be made from the other side of the river, he was
startled by the twinkle of a light in front and a little
to the left.

" That means Indians," was his conclusion, stopping short and peering intently; " they were wise enough to start their fire so far back that no one can possibly see it from the river."

In truth, it was so far from where he had halted, that he caught only the star-like flicker among the vegetation. He could not go back without investigating further. It was not impossible that he would pick up information of more moment than that which had fallen to Jo Spain.

Step by step, often pausing, looking around in the darkness, and intently listening, he advanced until barely fifty feet separated him from the fire, which was burning in a natural hollow in the wood. Before that fact was noted, the young man had found himself in the vicinity of a remarkable scene.

Around the camp-fire were gathered fully thirty Ottawa warriors. Some were seated on the ground, while a fallen tree bore the weight of one-third the number. There were no signs of food having been prepared, and, with one or two exceptions, the Indians were smoking their long-stemmed pipes. In the middle of the group stood a notable looking red-man, addressing those around him. He had flung aside his blanket, for the night, it will be remembered, was sultry, and the upper part of his body was bare, but painted, like his face, with varying colors.

There was no excitement in his manner, such as is shown by a dusky orator when trying to rouse his warriors to the fighting point. These savages were already keyed to that pitch, and required no urging to hold them there. He appeared to be giving directions, so as to prevent any mistake in the project in hand.

It did not require a second glance by Asher Norris to identify the leader. He had seen and spoken with him many a time, when all was peaceful around Detroit, and Major Gladwyn refused to believe the warnings that repeatedly came to him from different sources.

" That 's Pontiac; he looks just as he did when he came to Detroit last winter, and told the major that bad people were speaking lies in his ears, and that he would always be the brother of the white men. And all that time, and for a long while before, he was planning to destroy every post in the West."

In the stillness of the night, so profound that not even the soft murmur of the river reached him, the listener could hear every word said by the chieftain, but since it was in the Ottawa tongue, he was unable to comprehend a sentence. Norris had never taken the trouble to acquire the Indian lingo, while Jo Spain, the ranger, not only possessed, as we have stated, a peculiar aptitude in that direction, but,

PONTIAC AND HIS WARRIORS.

Page 48.

like every man serving under Major Rogers, he took pains to learn all that he possibly could of the language of his enemies. That knowledge had stood him too well many a time for him to neglect any opportunity. Thus it came about, as already shown, that he could talk Ottawa like a native, and could make himself understood in fully half a dozen aboriginal languages.

The decision of Norris was that Pontiac was instructing his followers in the special means to be used in attacking the schooner. Some of his gestures confirmed this suspicion, for he pointed several times in the direction of the vessel. His warriors nodded their heads in approval, some grunted, and the majority puffed deliberately at their pipes.

The belief was natural that all the Ottawas that were to take part in the attack were gathered in this camp, listening to their leader. It would hardly be supposed that those present were in more need of instruction than others; but this supposition of the youth, unfortunately, was wide of the truth.

" There are about thirty of them; some are in one another's way, so I can't make sure. Jo says there are others across the river, so that we shall be attacked by more than half a hundred redskins— that 's certain. They have rifles and knives, and when Pontiac leads them they will fight like so many furies. I don't see that there 's anything more for

4

me to learn by staying here, so I 'll go back and tell the captain how things look on Fighting Island.''

It was not likely that the Ottawas were in fear of any interruption from eavesdroppers, but their custom of keeping sentinels on guard caused Asher Norris to use the most extreme caution in withdrawing from the dangerous neighborhood, and it was well he did so, for within the space of a few minutes he was involved in an unexpected and most peculiar peril.

CHAPTER VI.

"BLOW HER UP, JACK!"

THE extreme care taken by Asher Norris in withdrawing from the vicinity of the Ottawa campfire made his progress of necessity very slow. So guarded was his approach that fully two hours had elapsed when he turned his back on the scene and step by step made his way toward Detroit river. Probably half the distance was passed when he paused and looked around. His keen eyes saw nothing but impenetrable darkness. Not the first twinkle of a campfire was visible.

"That's mighty strange," he said to himself, " for I am sure that when I first caught sight of it I was nearer the river than now. Jo has told me that when the Indians are about to break camp at night they sometimes smother the fire, so as to leave no traces that can be seen in the darkness. It looks as if they had done something of this kind. If so, then they must be moving toward the water—"

The thought had hardly assumed shape in his mind when a guttural exclamation was answered by several others. All came from a point between him and the Indian camp, and only a few yards distant. Beyond a doubt, the Ottawas, under the lead of Pontiac, were advancing to the Detroit river, over precisely the same course he had taken, and were almost literally treading on his heels.

It was a startling situation, and it seemed to Asher that his hair rose on end. If he turned to the right or left he would have to move so briskly that he was certain to be heard by these keen-eared red-men. If he continued toward the river they would soon overtake him, for to attempt to travel faster was to reveal his presence, and yet something must be done and on the instant.

The hands with which he was groping his way encountered the shaggy bark of an oak. The trunk was large enough to screen his body, and, stepping close behind it, he stood erect, interposing it as a shield between him and his enemies and praying that they would go by without discovering him.

No human being, or bird, or animal, for that matter, has the faculty of seeing where there is no light at all to assist vision. In this blank gloom the Ottawas must depend mainly upon the sense of feeling to avoid unpleasant collisions. They would grope deftly here and there, touching everything in their path of travel.

Thus it came about while the young man was listening to the bird-like rustling on the leaves made

by the moccasins, he heard the impact of a warrior's
hand against the bark on the other side of the tree
trunk which was sheltering him. The gentlest touch
was sufficient, and, swerving slightly to one side, he
moved on, the whole party drawing near the river
like so many phantoms.

Asher waited until some minutes after he was
sure every one of the shadows had passed. Then he
followed after them, so fearful of overtaking and
mingling with the party that he turned to the left,
so that when he finally reached the river's bank, it
was at a point considerably removed from where he
had landed.

The impressive feature about this strange business
was that everything thus far passed in complete
silence. But for what his eyes had told him and
what he had learned during his life at his home on a
frontier post, he would have found it hard to believe
that any living person beside himself was within a
mile of the spot. And yet there was a formidable
band of warriors under the leadership of one of the
great Indians of history, completing, if they had
not already completed, their preparations for attacking the schooner anchored in mid-stream, whose
scant but dauntless crew were as much veiled from
sight as were their deadly enemies.

Like the veteran ranger, the young man had
formed the belief that the blow would not be struck

until the night was well past, but it looked now as if
the dusky raiders were so confident of success that
they did not intend to wait.   Be all this as it might,
Asher was anxious above all things to get back to
the vessel, not only to warn Captain Horst and his
men (hardly necessary), but to give help in the
defence, which was certain to be of the most desperate nature.

Accordingly, he started to wade out in the water,
but had taken only a couple of steps when he
dropped into an unsuspected hole, which drew him
under the surface with a splash.   Believing that his
mishap would quickly bring some of the warriors to
the spot, he swam as far as he could under water,
and when forced to rise for breath dived again, so
that when he rose a second time he was beyond
sight of any one on the bank.

Like his uncle, he was now obliged to follow his
judgment alone, as to the location of the schooner.
He knew that he was below it, and, swimming until
near the middle of the stream, he headed up the
current and put forth all of the remarkable skill at
his command.

Asher Norris gained a vivid reminder of the perils
of a reconnoissance against a party of hostiles.
Suddenly something loomed to sight directly ahead
of him.   He " backed water " until he could make
out what it was, for he knew it was not the vessel.

It was an Indian canoe, and there was a second and a third. Evidently the occupants had not seen him, though he had not been swimming in absolute silence. So wonderfully fine was the action of the Ottawa paddles that only when the young man's ears were below the surface could he catch the soft rippling through the better conductor of sound. That party's approach to the sloop would never be discovered through the sense of hearing.

Since the canoes were moving diagonally in the same direction as Asher, he now did that which he would not have dared to do under less urgent necessity. Sheering to the left he took partly the same course, determined, if the thing were possible, to reach his friends before the danger burst upon them.

In this he was fortunately successful. While still feeling his way, as may be said, the familiar outlines assumed form in the darkness, and the next minute he was under the stern and climbing aboard by means of the rudder.

" Is Uncle Jo here ? " he asked in an excited whisper.

" I reckon I am," answered that individual, who, with Captain Horst, stood ready to fire upon him, in case he proved to be some one else.

" I am glad of it, for there 's the mischief to pay."

" Bein' as how we 've had a 'spicion of something

of the kind for some time, I might ask if that 's all the news you bring."

Asher Norris showed his training by proceeding to draw the charge from his rifle and reloading it, while talking to his relative, the captain, and the mate, the others holding their places, so as to avert a surprise. Jo Spain, who had found his way back to the boat with considerable difficulty some time before, had taken the same precaution.

" But Pontiac and his men are on the river; I saw their canoes only a few minutes ago."

This was news, and the ranger ceased his bantering manner. He asked his nephew to tell all that he had learned, and Asher did so as briefly as possible.

" You were right," said Captain Horst, " they are on both sides of us, and when they attack it will be from all directions."

" They are not on the sides of the stream," corrected Asher, " but on the stream itself; don't forget that."

" You seed only three canoes; they 've come out to look around; it 's too airly for the varmints to open bus'ness."

" We can't be sure of that."

" What 's the odds ?   One time will suit us as well as another—sh ! "

A tremulous, bird-like call, such as the ranger had

noticed earlier in the evening, was heard by every one on the schooner.

" That seems to be from the bank over there," whispered the mate.

" It is n't from the bank, but from the river; the boy is right; the varmints will attack us inside the next ten minutes. Pontiac thinks he has an easy thing of it, but it won't be the first mistake he 's made."

Nothing was to be gained by further talk, and the men separated, stationing themselves here and there along the sides and at the bow and stern of the schooner, so that no point was left unguarded. The ranger, who seemed naturally to assume the position of captain or director by virtue of the peculiar circumstances, did not stand still, but moved back and forth among the men, warning them to be on the alert, and to fire at the first moving object they discovered in the water.

The same keenness of attention enabled every one on board to hear the answering whistle from the direction of the left bank, followed a minute later by several calls from as many different points of the compass. There could be no doubt that Pontiac's plan was working to perfection.

Jo Spain had hardly reached the prow of the vessel when he saw one of the men bring his rifle to his shoulder. Instead of asking the meaning of the action, the ranger glanced out on the river, where he was able to discern something that looked like a canoe, but it was hovering on the very edge of invisibility, so that even his eyes could not be certain.

Nothing was said, but the man kept his weapon levelled, and the next moment pulled the trigger. No outcry followed, and when he lowered his piece and leaned forward to peer into the gloom, the object, whatever it was, had vanished.

" 'T was a good shot, Jim, all the same," said Jo; " and for all the varmint did n't yell, I should n't be 'sprised if you hit him. It 's my idee——"

The words were cut short by the discharge of a rifle from the stern, having been fired, indeed, by Captain Horst. Jo started hurriedly in that direction, but when half-way along the taffrail looked over the river and saw several canoes approaching the sloop with the speed of swallows. It was the same on the other side, at the bow and stern, and, indeed, from all points of the compass.

The Indians had moved silently about with their canoes until the vessel was actually surrounded, and then, at a signal from Pontiac, they all headed toward the schooner. They understood the ways of white men well enough to know that one or two of their number would be on guard, but they probably expected to board and capture the boat before the rest of the crew could be aroused and brought to the defence.

The woful mistake made by Asher Norris (and partly shared by Jo Spain) was in believing that not many more than fifty Indians would make the attack. It is a historical fact that the assailants of the schooner *Gladwyn*, on that sultry August night in 1763, were more than three hundred in number. The shadowy canoes seemed to cover the river and to dart forward from every point of the compass. It was impossible to tell from what quarter the main attack was made, except that it was from every quarter.

The ranger sprang forward, and, seeing that the single cannon could not miss, touched it off. Its thunderous report awoke the echoes along shore and was followed by a series of screeches and a splashing in the water, which told that it had done frightful execution. Had the number of assailants been what it was suspected, this probably would have checked them, and given the defenders a chance to reload their rifles, but the next minute the hordes were swarming over bow, stern, and sides, their knives in their teeth, and eager for the massacre.

With clubbed guns and with knives and hatchets, the white men fought with the fury of desperation. They knew that defeat or capture meant not simply death, but intolerable torture. The shouts and cries of the combatants made hideous the night.   Many of the assailants were struck down on the deck, and did not rise again.   Several of the defenders also fell, Captain Horst being the first man slain.   When his voice became silent, and his figure lay motionless, the others struggled more furiously than ever. In a brief while the slain Indians were double the number of white men, and yet with so many it effected nothing in the way of repulse.

Mate Jacobs was as cool as he was brave.   He awaited the critical moment, which speedily came. Resistance was hopeless, and he called out in a ringing voice:

"BLOW HER UP, JACK!"

CHAPTER VII.

WAITING FOR DAYLIGHT.

WHO would have suspected that the last, desperate, despairing command of Mate Jacobs to one of his men would be the means of saving the schooner ? Yet such was the fact.

Jack Carson, the sailor, who heard the words, ran forward with the intention of firing the magazine and blowing the vessel to atoms, but before he reached the spot he stopped, transfixed by a remarkable scene.

Among the Indians that had obtained possession of the deck were several Wyandots who understood English and knew the meaning of the order of the mate. They saw that if they remained another minute they and their companions would be hurled into eternity. They shouted a warning, and the same moment leaped as far out into the river as they could, and swam with might and main, diving and diving again in the furious effort to get as far as possible from the schooner before the explosion came. In a twinkling, as may be said, not an Indian was left on board the *Gladwyn*.

The defenders could hardly credit their senses. The retreat was as sudden as the attack. In one second all hope was gone, and in the next second the peril had departed.

But there could not be such savage fighting without some sad consequences. Of the crew, two had been killed during the fight, and four were seriously wounded. Of the Indians, seven were killed and twenty wounded, and it is known that eight of the latter died within a brief time. As has been stated, Captain Horst was the first one of the defenders to fall, the other being a member of the crew. Jo Spain was hurt, though he made light of his injury, while Asher Norris was one of the six gallant defenders who did not receive a scratch.

The dead and wounded were tenderly looked after, but the fear of a renewal of the attack kept the rest on the alert. The single cannon was recharged to the muzzle, and each rifle placed ready for instant use, while the unhurt men moved here and there on the watch for the first appearance of their enemies.

" I never dreamed that my order to Jack to blow up the schooner would have that effect," said Mate Jacobs to Jo Spain, after they had partly recovered from the flurry. " It's a pity I did n't try it before poor Captain Horst went down."

" It come about 'cause some of the varmints

knowed what you meant by the words; a redskin don't care any more 'bout bein' lifted among the clouds by gunpowder than we do."

" Do you fancy they will try it again ? "

" Not if we keep the right sort of watch; they 'll be pryin' 'round purty soon to see if we 're of the 'pinion that we can afford to go to sleep over it, which the same observation reminds me, as it were——"

And with this remark, the ranger brought his long, formidable rifle to his shoulder, took the best aim he could in the darkness, and pressed the trigger.

As the spiteful crack rang out over the water it was echoed by a screech that left no doubt of its effect.

" I did n't see anything out there," observed Asher Norris, looking toward the point at which the weapon had been aimed. " Was he in a canoe ? "

" No; he was n't fool 'nough for that; he was swimmin'; I 'm s'prised that he should try it so soon after the scrimmage; but he won't do so no more. As I was obsarvin' when that varmint broke in on me, they don't want to let us slip away, now that we 've scooped in so many; they know, too, that we 've a lot of powder on board, and Pontiac wants to get it mighty bad."

" Do you think he was among the assailants ? "

" Do I think so ? I know it. I could tell his voice in a thousand; it was too dark to see very plain, but I catched sight of the chap. He climbed up over the bow, and was one of the fust on deck. Pontiac aint no coward; I tried my best to get at him, but there was so many atween us, and things were so interestin' like, that I could n't get ahead very fast. I think he knowed me after a bit, and he was as eager to get at me as I was to reach him. So we both set out to do that, which the same bein' so, we worked along the deck purty fast, till we was almost within reach, and then——"

" Well ? "

" Jacobs sung out, ' Blow her up, Jack! ' There never was a worse scared Injin than Pontiac at them words. He did n't need anybody to tell him what they meant, fur the rapscallion knows English as well as he knows Ottawa, and he made one big jump as if he expected to land up among the limbs of the trees on the island over there, and that was the last of him."

So hurried had been the flight of the assailants that, contrary to the custom of their people, they left such as were killed on the deck, four in number, where they fell. The bodies were flung overboard. The startling cry of the mate so wrought upon the badly wounded that they forgot their hurts for the moment and plunged overboard with the others, though, as we have stated, quite a number did not survive.

It was certainly singular that any one of the Indians should have expected to find the white men off their guard after the exciting events a short time before, but the severe lesson given by the ranger produced a wholesome effect. They were not likely to repeat the experiment for some time to come.

Jo did not hold one position. He passed back and forth over the deck, pausing here and there to peer out into the gloom, while his anxiety to hear the slightest noise caused him to speak in a whisper. The bird-like calls from one shore to another left no doubt that the hostiles were signaling to one another, and the ranger knew that if the least invitation were given the attack would be renewed in overwhelming numbers. The crew was weak enough in the first place, but it was now so much weaker that hardly a moment's stand could be made against the rush. It was the dread of the blowing up of the schooner—that, and nothing else—which kept the Ottawas and their friends at bay.

At the end of an hour, to the surprise of every one, a slight breeze made itself felt. It was hardly to be hoped that it would hold, but the mate ordered the sails set, so that no possible advantage should be lost. The anchor having been lifted, the soft rippling at the bow showed that the schooner

5

was actually moving in the direction of Fort Detroit.

The progress, however, was very gentle, and the breeze carried the craft less than a fourth of a mile when it died away altogether. Still in the hope that it might be renewed, Captain Jacobs—as he might now be considered—allowed the sails to stand and kept the anchor raised. Strange it was that even such a veteran as Jo Spain did not suspect the peril this was liable to bring upon them.

Surrounded by the deep gloom, with both shores invisible, and no stars or moon in the sky, the captain and crew did not suspect, what was the fact, that the schooner was drifting and actually losing way. It was farther down stream than when the anchor was hoisted.

The gravest of consequences might have followed from this blunder, but for its detection through an unexpected occurrence. It will be remembered that there was a moon in the sky, though its light was shut out by the mass of clouds which overspread and filled the heavens, but by and by there came a partial lightening. The gibbous orb showed for a moment at the ragged opening between two expanses of vapor, only to vanish immediately.

" Wal, I 'll be shot ! " exclaimed the ranger to the captain ; " drop the anchor, quick ! "

The order was promptly given and obeyed. Then

Jacobs asked the meaning of the hunter's exclamation.

" There aint more 'n twenty yards atween us and
Fightin' Island ! "

" Great heavens ! " replied the captain; " I was
sure that if we were n't going forward, we were
holding our own; it 's a bad place for us to be, and
I 'll let the sails stand, so if there comes a cat's-paw
we can use it."

Just then the moon seemed to flirt some of the
obstructing clouds from before her face, and every
man saw that Jo had spoken the truth.   There were
the deep gloomy trees, seemingly so close that one
could have tossed a biscuit among them.

" The worst of this infernal business is," added Jo,
" that the varmints will find it out mighty sudden."

" They will not dare to board us."

" There won't be any need of it; they 'll just
stand back among the trees and let drive as they get
the chance, and there 'll be plenty of chances."

It was a most uncomfortable situation, but the
sagacious ranger had the remedy to offer.   It probably was the fact that their enemies were unaware
of the new peril of the schooner, but they would
not remain long in ignorance.   If the *Gladwyn* were
there when the sun rose, some, if not all, of the
crew would be picked off.   She must get nearer
the middle of the broad river if she would escape.

Three of the crew stepped softly into the small boat at the stern, which had not been harmed during the conflict. There were three pairs of oars, which they took in hand. Pointing the bow toward the left shore, they rowed with might and main, while the remainder stood with guns ready to use the instant a sight was caught of any of the Indians.

It will be remembered that the schooner was a small one, and she speedily felt the tugging at her side. The heavy bow slowly swung out stream, and she began moving at a snail's pace through the water.

It was important that the mistake should not be made of going too far, for there were no landmarks to guide, and in their eagerness they might cross over to the western bank.

" That 'll do," suddenly called Jo, in a guarded voice; " hurry back, boys ! "

It seemed to Captain Jacobs that they had not gone far enough, but he accepted the view of the ranger, who pronounced their escape one of the most remarkable he had known.

" We was a lot of fools that we did n't think of it," he said, " but I make no doubt that we 're a confounded nearer Fort Niagara, and consequently farther from Detroit than we was when we had the row with Pontiac and the rest of the varmints. Now when you let the anchor drop agin, we 'll 'low it stay there till sun up, no matter if a hurricane knocks things stiff.''

No one felt a disposition to sleep. Their experience had been too frightful, while the presence of the two cold and motionless bodies and of the wounded men was a forceful reminder of what had taken place but a short time before and what, despite the extraordinary escape of the rest, was possible might occur again.

There had been a moment when all expected to plunge into eternity together, but having survived, the longing for life returned, though sooner than surrender or submit to capture, the torch would be applied to the magazine. At any rate, everything depended upon unremitting vigilance, and that was maintained through the long solemn hours which intervened between the repulse and daylight.

Again the faint, far-away report of a gun came through the arches of the forest, followed by the cry of the night-hawk and the bark of the fox. The occasional breaking of the clouds overhead gave fitful glimpses of the smooth, silent river, and once when the face of the moon was entirely clear, the faint outline of the shore on the left loomed out of the darkness, quickly to vanish again.

Strange that for hours not a sight or sound was gained of the redmen who had raged so fiercely, filling the night with their wild cries and their fierce endeavor to slay those that had never done them harm.

" Jo," said the captain, calling the ranger to the stern of the vessel, " there 's something the matter with the rudder."

" How ? "

" It does n't move freely."

" Some of the varmints clum up that way, and it might be they knocked it askew."

" I hardly think that, but it 's near daylight, and we shall soon find out what it means."

When the gray mist of morning began stealing over forest and river, the two looked curiously down from the stern of the vessel at the old-fashioned steering apparatus which was moved by a long curved tiller.

The upper part of the rudder projected slightly above the surface of the water, and, balanced across it, face downwards, with his head and shoulders on one side and the lower part of his body and legs on the other, was an Indian warrior that had long been dead, lying just as he had fallen hours before.

The ranger stepped carefully down and turned the face so that both could see the features. " Umph! I thought so," he exclaimed.

It was all that was left of Red Feather, the Iroquois.

CHAPTER VIII.

THE ABSENT ONE.

BEFORE it was fairly light, the wind sprang up anew, the anchor was hoisted and, the sails of the schooner, catching the impulse, carried the vessel up the river toward the fort of Detroit. In a short time Fighting Island was left to the south, and the open stream lay before them all the way to the post and to Lake St. Clair beyond.

Now that the *Gladwyn* had escaped from the overwhelming attack, there was well-grounded fear that it would be annoyed in an equally treacherous manner. With that dread of the blowing up of the vessel in the last emergency, it was not believed that the assault would be repeated, for since the defenders could detect any approach before the hostiles were within striking distance, thus enabling them to use the small cannon and their comparatively numerous rifles several times before coming to close quarters, the Indians would shrink from the risk, leaving out of consideration the other fear of being involved in the blowing up of the craft.

Accordingly, Jo Spain instructed the crew to keep

as much out of sight as possible. That the advice was wise was proved more than once, when shots were fired from both shores, the bullets whistling startlingly close. The ranger, who was on the watch, caught sight of a Wyandot, more reckless than his companions, who stood out in full view on a small clearing, and deliberately pointed his gun at Jo, who was just as prominent on the deck of the schooner. But the white man was more prompt in sighting and pulling trigger. As a consequence, the warrior's bullet went wild, and since that of the ranger sped true, no more need be added.

A few miles above Fighting Island, the schooner came in sight of the French houses which lined the eastern bank of the river from a mile below the fort to almost the same distance above, Detroit standing on the opposite or western shore. About half-way between the upper and lower ends of the fringe of French cabins and directly back of them, was the camp of the Wyandots. Farther north and above a point opposite the post and also back of the cabins was the camp of the Ottawas, while that of the Pottawatomies was on the western shore, just below Detroit.

" We 'll catch it from both sides," remarked Jo Spain, as they approached the last-named camp, " and we must lay low."

It was well that all hands followed his advice.

The schooner was near mid-channel, going smoothly forward, when fully a hundred warriors, dancing about and furiously shrieking, opened a rattling fire, which was kept up until the vessel passed beyond range. The bullets pattered against the hull, the masts, and the cabin and elevated portions of the vessel, cut through the sails, and skipped and pattered in the water beyond. The precaution of the men saved them from harm.

Only a short distance above and on the other shore was the village of the Wyandots, where the performance was repeated. Captain Jacobs set the rudder, and the remainder of the crew made sure they were protected, so that good fortune again attended them. Then the schooner swung over toward the western bank, and came to anchor under the protection of the guns of the fort.

The arrival of the vessel was an event in the history of the siege of Detroit. In the sultry stillness of the preceding night, the reports of the guns down the river had been plainly heard, and Major Gladwyn and his garrison hardly dared to hope that any of the crew had escaped. Their fears became despair, when one of the French residents, most of whom were secretly friendly to the Americans, came over about daybreak with word that a Wyandot runner had just told him that the schooner had been captured and all on board slain. And here was the vessel herself.   True, she brought two dead and four seriously wounded, but that was better than was expected.   Besides, the supply of powder was most welcome, for the ammunition was already running low, because of the vigorous defence required by the incessant attacks of Pontiac and his men.   The dead were tenderly buried, and the injured attended with such care that after a time all fully recovered from their grievous wounds.

Jo Spain was the brother of Mrs. Peggy Norris, the mother of Asher, and she and her husband gave the brave ranger joyous welcome.   It was because of these connections that Jo, when he accompanied Major Rogers westward to receive the surrender of Detroit, remained at the post, instead of returning eastward with that famous Indian fighter.

A gentler and warmer welcome awaited the son at the hands of his parents.   Some faint idea, perhaps, may be formed of the anguish of the father and mother when they heard the sounds of firing during the impressive stillness of the night, and, while not certain, they still had reason to believe that their only child was on board the imperiled schooner. And here, too, he was, with his sturdy arms around the neck of each in turn, and without so much as a scratch to tell of the frightful ordeal through which he had passed.

Several weeks had passed since the departure of

the son, and as he looked around the palisaded inclosure very few and slight changes caught his eye. The little wooden houses were arranged with no regard to symmetry or appearance, and a conflagration once started among them would lay all in ashes. But the sentinels were alert, the cannon were kept fully charged, and whenever a hostile stole up within range the chances were that he would be riddled before he could get away. A number of outbuildings, which gave the assailants good shelter, and from which they kept up for a time an annoying fire, had been set in flames by red-hot shot, and destroyed. All appearances promised that if the garrison could maintain a supply of food and ammunition they would be able to hold Pontiac at bay for an indefinite time.

It may be noted here as an interesting fact that the French settlers on the eastern shore of the Detroit river gave valuable aid to the beleaguered garrison. This, of necessity, was secret, for Pontiac would have visited ferocious punishment upon them had the knowledge come to him. Just before the chieftain made his famous visit to Major Gladwyn, at which he intended to massacre that officer and all the garrison, a number of warriors went to the French blacksmith and had their gun barrels filed off, so as to permit of their being hidden under their blankets. The blacksmith did not know the significance of the curious request made of him, but seeing something suspicious in it, sent word of the occurrence to Major Gladwyn. That, and the warning of Catherine, the Ojibwa girl, saved Detroit from being wiped from the face of the earth.

It finally became too dangerous for the French settlers to send anything to the garrison. The sagacious Pontiac may have been suspicious, for he passed through the settlement with a keener eye than usual. Besides, as the siege progressed, he needed supplies for his own warriors, and procured many of them from the French people. A singular fact was connected with this incident. The Ottawa chieftain in all cases where he took such supplies, gave his promissory notes in payment. These were scratched upon bark, and were probably the first dealings of that nature in which an American Indian took part. Nor must we omit to state that every one of the notes was afterward redeemed in full by their maker.

When the flurry following the arrival of the schooner had subsided and Asher Norris had exchanged greetings with most of his acquaintances, he strolled through the palisaded inclosure, as if he had no other object in mind than to while away time and to note the changes which, as we have said, were of trifling character. Such, we repeat, seemed to be his purpose, but in truth his errand was a definite one.

Near the southeast bastion was the home of Hugh Linwood, his wife and daughter, Madge, the last nearly two years younger than Asher. The couple were so young that the parents of neither suspected the tender feeling that was budding into life on the part of each. It may be doubted whether Asher or Madge suspected it. Asher only knew that the hazel eyes, the ruddy cheeks, the elastic figure, whose beautiful outlines could not be hidden by the dress of homespun, the wealth of black hair, the flashing teeth, and the sweet, winsome disposition, were never, he was confident, repeated anywhere else in this world, nor if repeated in the future, could they ever hold quite the charm for him that they did when they glowed in the face, form, and disposition of Madge Linwood.

And as for Madge's views, why, no one could deny that Asher was the handsomest, most manly, the bravest and best youth in Fort Detroit—aye, among all the frontier posts and the settlements. She had declared it herself (with blushes and tremulous eyes), and not one had ever dared to say her nay, for to do so would have been to utter a dreadful untruth—too dreadful, indeed, for any human being to brave its utterance.

And so it was that in the most natural manner in the world Asher Norris's footsteps halted in front of Hugh Linwood's cabin. The latchstring was hanging out, and, giving it a gentle twitch, the ponderous door swung inward, and he stepped across the threshold with a pleasant greeting to husband and wife. Hugh's turn to go on guard would not come for two or three hours. He was sitting in his heavy chair, smoking his pipe and looking rather gloomily into the wood fire burning on the hearth, while his wife was busy with her household duties.

The couple looked around as the sunlight streamed over the shoulders and head of the athletic youth, whose face brought still more genial and welcome sunshine into the homely room. Husband and wife had witnessed the arrival of the schooner, but, not knowing that Asher was on board, had returned to their home without staying to welcome the survivors.

Shaking hands with the two, Asher sat down and soon made them acquainted with his stirring experience of the night before. They listened with close attention and deep interest, but through it all Asher plainly saw that the couple were oppressed by some trouble of their own. That, and the fact that Madge was not in sight, sent a chill of apprehension through him.

Nothing would have been more natural than that she should be absent for the moment with some of the neighbors, for Madge was a favorite everywhere, and in case of illness or trouble she was a

ministering angel. Asher had hardly completed his
narrative when he looked sharply about the room
and asked:

" Where 's Madge ? "

His alarm intensified when both of the parents
sighed and the mother shook her head with a sup-
pressed moan. The father slowly puffed at his pipe
and stared into the glowing embers, as if his sorrow
was too deep for utterance. Asher wheeled about
in his chair, and, swallowing a lump in his throat,
and with a white, scared face, asked in a husky
voice:

" Is she dead ? "

" No, no, no," answered her father, " but what a
fool I have been; what a fool her mother was! Oh,
why were we so blind ? Woe is me ! Woe is
me ! "

He swayed his head, which sank low on his breast
and sighed as if his heart was breaking.

" But do you not mean to tell me ? Let me hear
the worst! " demanded the youth with tempestuous
impatience.

It seemed to strike the father just then that the
request of their visitor was reasonable.

" You know Pierre Muire, who lives on the other
side of the river, with his old mother, where in truth
they have lived ever since Pierre was born ? "

" Yes; I have known Pierre for years."

" You know how much his feeble old mother loved Madge ? "

" Of course; every one loves her. I have sometimes thought that Pierre loved her more than he had a right to."

The parents might have noticed this declaration, prompted as it was by a curious jealousy, had it been uttered at any other time, but it made no impression upon them now.

" Well, Pierre came over and said he was afraid his mother was dying. She asked as a last favor that Madge might go and see her. Madge was filled with sorrow, for she tenderly loved the old lady, and, yielding to her entreaties, we allowed her to go back with Pierre."

" When was that ? "

" Two nights ago."

" Where is she now ? "

" God only knows," was the heart-broken reply.

" WHERE IS SHE NOW ?"   *Page 80.*

CHAPTER IX.

MISSING.

SUPPRESSING, so far as he could, his alarm and impatience, Asher Norris pressed the parents of Madge Linwood for further particulars of her absence. They were not many and were speedily given.

Enough has been told to give the reader a fair idea of the peculiar situation of the several hundred French residents, whose cabins lined the other side of the Detroit river for a mile or more up and down stream. Since Pontiac was making war upon the Americans (or English, as they were termed at the time), who were the conquerors of the French, the latter were looked upon as friends by the hostile redmen.

The French Canadians endeavored on their part to maintain the position of neutrality, and it may be said that they succeeded to a great extent in doing so. Naturally the sympathy of the majority was with those of their own race, even though the two nations were rivals, and it has been shown that when it was safe to carry important information or food to the fort, the Frenchmen were not lacking to do it.

It must be confessed, however, that among the settlers were a number who held so consuming a hatred of their masters that they eagerly helped the cruel Ottawa leader. As an illustration, when Major Dalzell set out some weeks before to attack Pontiac's camp, that chieftain was warned by some of the French of the intended blow. Thus apprised, he made his preparations so complete that he inflicted the most shocking massacre of the siege upon that brave body of men.

Until the surrender of Detroit the French (also known as Canadians) and few American settlers were on the best of terms. They visited back and forth and intermarriages took place. Madge Linwood was fond of paddling across the river in her small canoe and spending days and nights with her friends on the other shore. Among those to whom she became deeply attached was the aged Mrs. Muire, who had been a widow and an invalid for several years, and whose son was considerably older than Asher Norris.

The siege naturally changed all this. It was perilous for any American or Englishman to appear among the French settlements, for he was liable to be discovered by the hostiles, who would show him scant mercy. The risk was less for a Frenchman to visit Detroit, for no one there would harm him, but. Major Gladwyn could not make such callers wel-

come. It was impossible to forget the lesson of
Bloody Ridge, and he was always suspicious of these
persons, no matter how friendly they had been in
the past. It cannot be denied that he had good
ground in many instances for his misgivings.

Among the very few whom he fully trusted was
Pierre Muire. That young man had helped to bring
food to the garrison, and crossed the river one night
in a blinding storm, to warn the commandant of
Pontiac's intention of destroying both schooners by
means of fire rafts.

Curious as it may seem, the faith of Pontiac in
the young man seemed equally complete as that of
Major Gladwyn. This was proof of the mental
acuteness of the young Frenchman. Appalling
would be the punishment of the Ottawa leader
should he learn the truth, while the opportunity to
administer such punishment was within reach. Such
was the situation when Pierre Muire paddled across
the river, being unhesitatingly admitted within the
palisades, made his way to the cabin of Hugh Linwood, with the statement that his mother was at the
point of death, and her last wish was that she might
feel the cool, gentle pressure of Madge's hand upon
her brow and the touch of her sweet lips before she
passed away.

The request was so pathetic that the parents were
hardly less touched than their child, but in their

sympathy the father did not lose sight of prudence to the complete extent that his lamentations to Asher Norris implied. He took his visitor aside and asked him whether it was safe for Madge to go back with him. She had not been across the river since the siege began. She was known not only to Pontiac himself, but to many of his warriors, and it would be characteristic of the race to strike her father through his child.

Pierre Muire seemed to be honest when he replied that nothing would induce him knowingly to take Madge into danger. He was the friend of Pontiac, or rather Pontiac looked upon him as such, and no one would dare harm him, or a hair of the head of any of his friends.

So it came about that just as it was growing dusk, Madge entered the canoe of Pierre, who, swinging the paddle like an Indian, sent the light craft skimming swiftly toward the eastern bank. He had promised that, no matter what the condition of his aged parent was, he would return with Madge on the following night, at about the same hour that he had left the post. While he believed it was safe for him to do this when the sun was shining, he made use of the darkness as an additional precaution.

The second night had come and gone, and nothing was seen or a whisper heard of Madge or him who took her away.

With the passing of every hour the misgiving and grief of the couple increased, until they were in the depth of anguish, when Asher Norris called and learned the truth from them.

Hugh Linwood berated himself and wife, and she did the same in a less degree, because they had consented to the foolhardy proposal. Asher, in his own mind, was equally severe in condemning them, but regrets and remorse could do no good. They must do something, or give up and helplessly await the issue of events.

The intolerable feature in the whole thing was that it looked as if nothing could be accomplished to solve the mystery or to help Madge. The most hopeful view was that, after she had reached the Muire home, and was ready to return, Pierre had found it more dangerous than he suspected, and was waiting for a better opportunity. They hoped that he would present himself on the coming night. If he failed to do so, utter despair would overwhelm them.

Asher Norris did not dare tell all the thoughts that surged through his brain, for to do so would only add to the anguish of the stricken parents. Possibly, after all, he was wrong. One terrible thought was this:

" I don't believe that old Mrs. Muire is ill, or at any rate any more so than she has been for years.

Pierre has long been in love with Madge.   She does n't suspect it, nor does any one else beside Pierre except myself.   I have noticed his eyes when he looked ready to devour her.   He has seen that she is fond of me, and has made up his mind that if he does n't get her away pretty soon he will never be able to do so.

"So he formed his plan.   He intends to take her over to his home, as he has done, and keep her there under the plea that there 's too much risk to attempt to bring her back for a good while to come.   Or——

"He started last night, according to promise, and has fallen into the hands of the Indians, with all that that implies."

But there lay the trouble, for the fact might imply one of several things.   It might be that by some means Pontiac had learned that Pierre was a spy against him and had seized and put him to death.

It might be that Pierre was really a spy for Pontiac, and was a subtle foe of the garrison (somehow or other this theory struck Asher Norris as the most probable), and that the betrayal of Madge was part of a deep-laid scheme for placing her in such peril that she would give any pledge the Frenchman asked for the sake of life and liberty.

It might be that there was even more behind all this, which as yet Asher did not grasp; but he could not shut out the belief that whatever the issue of the dreadful business, the treachery and guilt of Pierre Muire would be established.

But speculation might go on for hours, with no certainty of the truth being reached. The one great question was, What, if anything, could be done to help the absent one ? Only one reasonable scheme presented itself.

Jo Spain, the ranger, spoke French like a native. He might visit the settlement in the character of a Frenchman, and learn the truth. There would be considerable risk, for he would be recognized by many of the people who knew him well, not to mention Pontiac and a number of warriors. If Pierre Muire should prove a true friend he would give the ranger shelter; but if an enemy, there would be a speedy end to the adventurous career of the scout.

" I have been figuring ever since morning," said Hugh Linwood, after Asher had made known his plan of intrusting the work to Jo Spain, " what it was I could do to help Madge. It 's hard to restrain myself from jumping into one of the boats and paddling across the river to Muire's house."

" And you could do nothing worse; you are known to every one there as a member of the garrison, and your life would n't be worth a minute's purchase."

" I suppose so, and it is the same with you."

Unconsciously the parent touched a sensitive chord, for in and out of the thoughts of Asher Nor-

ris ran the question whether it was not possible for
him to strike a blow for the one who seemed to
become tenfold dearer now that she was lost. It
would be folly for him to try to figure out that there
was hope for him and none for the elder man. All
the same, however, he disliked to be reminded thus
forcibly of the truth.

" Jo won't hesitate, when the situation is told to
him," said Asher. " Do my father and mother
know anything about it ? ".

" They have learned nothing from me."

" It 's as well; Jo can't make any move before
night, and I suppose he will want to meet lots of his
friends before he goes."

Asher saw that neither of the parents suspected
Pierre Muire of any wrong intention, and he was
wise in deciding not to raise any doubt in their
minds, for it could do no good and would only add
to their anguish. It would be time enough for
them to know the truth when it could not be hidden
any longer.

When it came time for Linwood to resume military duty, Asher accompanied him from his house,
while the wife went to visit a sympathizing neighbor.

Captain Jacobs had made his report to Major
Gladwyn, and the powder and few supplies were
stowed away beyond the reach of the hostiles clam-
oring for the lives of the defiant garrison. Sorrow-

ing over the deaths of Captain Horst and one of the
crew, there was rejoicing because of the decisive
repulse of the assailants and the heavy loss inflicted
upon them.

Just as Asher Norris reached his own threshold,
he received word that Major Gladwyn wished to see
him. The youth lost no time in repairing to the
quarters of the commandant, wondering what the
business could be.

The officer merely wished to hear Asher's account
of his visit to Fighting Island during the previous
evening.

"Spain has told me what he discovered on the
western shore and given me your account of what
you observed on the eastern bank, which happened
to be an island, but to make sure there is no mistake
I will be obliged if I can hear it from your lips."

The young man told the story with which the
reader has long since become familiar, the officer
listening with close attention.

"What strikes me as curious, is that all the Indians seen by you and Spain were less than a quarter
of those that attacked the schooner."

"I should say hardly one-sixth."

"And yet you saw and recognized Pontiac
haranguing his warriors. You would suppose that
he would have had all who were on that side of the
river gathered round him."

" I was sure of it at the time, but was mistaken."

" And the Iroquois, whom you were foolish enough to set ashore, were among the fiercest of your assailants. It might have been expected. I hope Spain will bring back some more valuable information."

" Has he left the post ? "

" He left about an hour ago."

" How long will he be gone ? "

" Not even he can say, but it will be for several days—perhaps for a week and possibly longer, for his errand is a very important one."

CHAPTER X.

THE KNIGHT TO THE RESCUE.

IT was with strange emotions that Asher Norris heard from Major Gladwyn the announcement that Jo Spain, the ranger, had left the post to be gone for a number of days. His feelings were not wholly of disappointment, for until then he had forced himself to believe that he was to bear no hand in the rescue of Madge Linwood—a belief which the reader will understand was a torturing one to him.

" Heaven intends that the work shall be done by me," was his reflection, and despite the almost hopeless prospect, he experienced a curious revival of spirits at the certainty that he was not to remain idle while she was in such imminent peril.

" I shall not sleep day or night until she is with her friends again."

All this we say was commendable and natural, but with " sober second thought," his enthusiasm suffered a dampening. It is easy for any person to form a resolution, but it is altogether another thing to carry it out. Having formed the determination, however, he meant that nothing should interfere with it.

He expected the first real trouble would be the opposition of his parents, but to his surprise and gratification, both father and mother commended his decision.

" It is a pity that Jo is gone beyond recall," said his father, " but it would be a still greater pity to leave Madge, without a person at the fort to raise his hand in her behalf. Go, my boy, and the blessing of God go with you."

He was sure of a similar Godspeed from the parents of Madge, but there again he was disappointed. While praising his chivalry, the couple pronounced it worse than hopeless, insisting that Asher would simply place himself in the greatest danger without being able to help, in the slightest degree, the missing one. The young man would not allow their despair to affect his resolution, but he agreed to wait until the night was well on before leaving the post. If Pierre Muire came back with Madge, he would be due shortly after dark.

Asher restrained his impatience until an hour after the time set, when he bade his friends good-by and hurriedly left the post, to enter upon the most remarkable experience of his life.

None knew better than he the location of Pierre Muire's home. It will be borne in mind that the long, thin line of French cabins extended along the eastern or opposite side of the river, from a point considerably above the fort to a point still farther down stream. Pierre lived near the upper end of the settlement, close to the Ottawa camp, directly behind it. Since Pontiac spent most of his time with his tribe, the youth would be compelled to approach close to his headquarters, and would run much risk of being seen and recognized by some of the warriors, if not by the terrible chieftain himself.

Instead of crossing the river directly from the fort, Norris entered his small canoe, which he was able to handle with the skill of an Ottawa or Ojibwa, and worked his way up the western bank, keeping close to the overhanging undergrowth, where, if hard pressed, he could leap to land and take advantage of the secure hiding offered. At the distance of barely a fourth of a mile was a small island lying near the eastern bank. By landing just below this island he would be almost among the settlers and within a stone's throw of the home of Pierre Muire.

It will be perceived that his purpose was to take up the search for Madge at the house which was her destination. If she were not still there, some of the neighbors would be able to give him the information necessary to push his search. He hoped, but hardly believed, that he would find the missing one in the cabin. With his judgment warped by jealousy, he partly suspected that Pierre had persuaded Madge to overstay her time.   It might be that his mother was so critically ill that the sympathetic girl was induced to remain longer with her, though to the ardent rescuer the conduct of Pierre Muire was beyond excuse or palliation.

In a short time the point was reached where Asher intended to turn the bow of his boat out into the channel and paddle for the eastern bank.   When ready to make the start he held the frail craft motionless, and with suspended paddle listened and peered around him into the all-enveloping gloom.

The night was similar in several respects to the preceding one.   It was close and sultry, with masses of clouds drifting across the sky and partly shading the rays of the moon, though not to the same extent as before.   This rendered the light treacherous and uncertain.   At times his keen vision was able to penetrate for fifty yards over the still water, and then, a few minutes later, he could see little more than the length of his canoe.

Looking across the river the lights in the cabins of the French settlers twinkled like stars low in the horizon, but it was blank darkness everywhere else. The palisades at Detroit were shut out by the intervening vegetation, and all seemed as gloomy, deserted, and silent as the tomb; nevertheless those sentinels had learned through the past months by dear experience the need of vigilance. The dusky scout could not steal up to the palisades to do harm without detection, and darkness offered no safer opportunity for attack than when the sun was at meridian.

The sounds that reached his ears served but to render the stillness more oppressive. The cry of the nighthawk, the whirr of a bird's wings as it shot past his boat, so near that he could have struck it with his paddle, the cry of the fox and wolf, the call of some man on the other bank to his neighbor, the soft murmur of the river, as it flowed onward on its long journey to the sea, the ripple of the current around a projecting root or dipping limb—all these were familiar, but this time they seemed a part of the " voice of silence " itself.

Asher was poised thus, with paddle balanced in his two strong hands, when a shiver suddenly passed through him, for barely ten feet distant, close to the bank behind him, sounded a loud splash, as if a man had plunged into the water and was swimming swiftly toward him. Like a flash Asher laid his paddle in the canoe and caught up his rifle.

The noise in the water showed that, whatever it was that had made the plunge, it was coming straight toward the canoe. Fortunately, before the brief distance was passed the moon came out from behind the obscuring clouds and revealed that, instead of a man, it was a huge bear that had set out to swim across the river.

Since the canoe was directly in the brute's course, and he showed no disposition to turn out for it, Norris dropped his gun and took up his paddle again.   One sweep was sufficient to send the craft several yards down stream, when he checked its progress and gave his attention once more to the bear.

Curiously enough, the latter also changed his course, and headed for the canoe and man, as if anxious to make a closer acquaintance.   It would have been easy for the youth to send a bullet through his brain, or by using his paddle, keep beyond reach of the clumsy animal.   But he did neither.   Waiting until he was almost at his side, and ready to thrust one of his enormous paws upon the gunwale of the canoe and overturn it, Norris raised the paddle aloft and brought down the end with a resounding whack upon the head of the bear.

The latter must have been astonished.   With a whiffing snort he swung round in the water, and instead of continuing across the river, made all haste to return to the shore which he had left but a few minutes before.   Norris heard him climb up the steep bank and shake his shaggy coat, after which he crashed off through the undergrowth.

Asher's reluctance to using his gun was the fear

that the brute was fleeing from some pursuer that was close upon him. The report, beside directing attention to himself, would leave the youth unprepared against the attack likely to follow; but the return of the bear to the point whence he came showed that he had not been escaping from an enemy, since the blow from the paddle would not have been likely so to obfuscate his soggy brain as to cause him to forget that important fact.

In obedience, however, to that habit of caution, most of which had been taught him by his uncle, Asher propelled the canoe a little farther up stream, when he again held it motionless, while he listened and looked around for other evidence of danger.

None appeared, and he yielded to the feeling of impatience, which had hardly been absent since leaving the post. Silently but swiftly he drove the boat across the river, heading slightly upward, so as to allow for the current. The twinkling lights on the other shore furnished guidance, but he would have found no difficulty had they been absent, since the dim light of the moon was sufficient to show him the way that had been familiar for many years.

But, as he neared the eastern bank, he slackened his speed, for every stroke took him closer to danger. It would not be strange if some of the Ottawas were passing in and out of the settlement, and possibly Pontiac himself was at the very spot

he had selected for a landing place.   In obedience
to an increasing misgiving, Norris headed up
stream, intending to land at the upper extremity of
the settlement.

It was at this critical juncture that the listening
ear caught the sound of paddles in the water.   The
fact that he was able to hear them proved that whoever occupied the boat was moving carelessly, as if
there was no cause for fear.   Some one had left the
shore near the place which he had selected for landing, and, judging from the sounds, was making for
the western bank.

Thus far the young man had learned from his
sense of hearing only.   The other boat was above
him, and farther out in the stream.   It had several
occupants, as was shown by the noise of the paddles.   Suddenly two tiny points of light appeared,
and, at the same moment, he caught the smell of
burning tobacco.   Two of the men in the boat were
smoking—another proof of their belief that there
was no cause for alarm.

These men might be Canadians, or they might be
Indians.   The only safe course was to accept them
as enemies, and Asher Norris did a thing which Jo
Spain would have complimented had he witnessed
it.   Glancing up at the sky, he saw that at that
moment the moon was emerging from a straggling
mass of vapor.   Already its reflection on the water

was increasing. A few seconds more and he was certain to be detected. With one silent sweep of the paddle he caused the canoe to dart like a swallow under into the ribbon of shadow which followed the windings of the shore.

This screened him from view while it revealed the larger boat so distinctly that he saw that it contained four persons, three of whom were swinging and swaying their paddles in true Indian fashion. It was the two at the rear that were smoking, but the obscurity prevented his distinguishing whether they were red or white men.

Again the sense of hearing came to his relief. One of the occupants spoke and another replied. The guttural grunt in each case removed the last doubt. The four were Indians.

While so near the eastern bank, where there was no cause for fear, it was not strange that two of these warriors indulged their taste for smoking, that three used their paddles carelessly, and that they did not hesitate to speak in their natural tones. But before the canoe sighted the western bank those pipes would be extinguished, the paddles would sway back and forth with the noiselessness of the seafowl fanning the thin air miles above the earth, and not a sound would come from the dusky lips. Where they were going and what was their errand was more than Asher Norris could conjecture, and he did not make the effort.   He had enough on his hands without giving thought to that.   He comprehended one thing: he had met with an exceedingly narrow escape, for had he been seen the others beyond a doubt would have called him to account.

But Norris was now at the end of his voyage. He groped his way along the bank for a few rods, listening and using his eyes as best he could, until he felt it useless to go farther.   So he turned the prow of his canoe abruptly to the right, and drove the nose hard against the bank.   Then stepping lightly forth, he drew it so far out of the water that there was no danger of its being carried away by the current.

At last he had reached the settlement, and was within a few rods of the home of Pierre Muire.

CHAPTER XI.

THE time had passed for caution. To crouch or endeavor to steal forward without attracting notice was the surest way to attract it. Asher Norris must conduct himself as if among friends.

There was nothing in the nature of a street to distinguish the French settlement that stretched along the eastern bank of Detroit river and contained several hundred people. All the cabins faced the water. There was the blacksmith shop, the trader's store, a small Catholic chapel, and other structures at varying distances apart. Most of the houses were surrounded by patches of crudely tilled ground, while here and there a couple of buildings almost touched each other. Numerous canoes resting against the bank showed how accustomed the inhabitants were to the water, from which they drew an important source of supply, though most of the men were voyageurs, trappers, and hunters, who were absent from home in the far-away forests for weeks and months at a time.

They lived in the primitive fashion of the early

pioneers, skins and furs forming the principal part of their garments, though with some there was a pretence to linen and woollen goods. Many of the cabins contained spinning-wheels, and there were numerous cattle, fowl, and domestic animals. Although in still earlier days oiled paper served for window-panes, there was no lack of glass at this French settlement, but the fire which burned on the hearth at night, even during the warm weather, gave the only illumination of the interior.

Because of the sultriness of the weather, most of the front doors were open, so that the light was thrown in front of the dwellings and across the winding path which led in front of them, and which Asher Norris was now following.

He was not the only one moving about. The hour was so late that most of the children were in bed, and the dogs, of which there were plenty, paid no heed to him. Since he was dressed like the Canadians and conducted himself like them, it is probable that in the obscurity the canines took him for a friend.

Sauntering forward seemingly in an indifferent manner, the visitor was on the alert and allowed nothing to escape his vision. He had but a few paces to go when he arrived opposite the Muire home. As he did so, he stopped short, with an involuntary exclamation. It was as dark as the tomb. He caught the murmur of voices from within, though the sound was heard only at slight intervals, as if people were holding partial converse.

While he stood in perplexity he heard a footstep behind him. The sky at that moment cleared, and, aided by the light from the nearest house at the rear, he saw as he turned his head that the one so near him was a Canadian.

"Heavens! is that you, Norris?" he asked in a scared undertone.

Asher recognized the speaker as Jean Chotean, who had visited the post several times, but of whose loyalty both he and Major Gladwyn were suspicious.

"Yes, Jean, it is I; I hope you are well," replied Norris, unconsciously lowering his voice.

"Why do you come here? Don't you know the danger?"

"I know there are some places safer."

"There could n't be any more dangerous; Pontiac gave orders yesterday that every Englishman found on this side of the river should be killed, no matter if he were sitting at one of our tables. He said if any of us saw a white man from the fort and failed to kill or make him prisoner, he would slay the one that dared disobey his command."

"Well, Jean, I am here; I suppose you must do your duty."

"If you mean by that that I shall betray you,

you are mistaken; but let me entreat you to get
away without a minute's delay."

" I shall not stay longer than necessary; but, tell
me, Jean, why is Pierre Muire's house dark and
closed ? "

" Have n't you heard ?   No; how could you ?
His mother is dead."

" Dead ! when did she die ? " asked the astonished Asher.

" This morning, shortly after daybreak."

" Where is Pierre ? "

" Nobody knows."

The Canadian shrugged his shoulders and partly
spread out his palms, as many Frenchmen do, for
he carried no rifle with him.

" What do you mean ? "

" Ah ! Pierre loved his mother—no son ever loved
mother more.   He has been crazed by his grief; he
has gone nobody can say where.   He may be at the
bottom of the river; he may have stood at the muzzle of his gun and kicked the trigger with his foot—
who shall say ?   We shall never see him again, of
that I am assured."

" When did he leave ? "

" Last night ! he had with him the daughter of
Hugh Linwood, the beauteous and charming Madge.
He brought her over to cheer his mother in her last
moments, but he had promised to take her home,

and he set out to do so, when it was hardly dark, and he has not been seen at his home since then.''

'' Then he was not with his mother when she passed away ? ''

'' Alas! how could he be, when she lingered until this morning, but it made no difference to the good woman.''

'' And why not ? ''

'' Her senses were gone—she knew no one, not even the priest that shrived her—so it was well,'' and Jean Chotean piously crossed himself.

'' And those are neighbors inside the house, keeping watch with the body.''

'' You are right; she is to be buried to-morrow.''

'' Whether or not her son returns ? ''

'' Have I not told you that the son will never return. He is dead.''

'' You have no right to say that, unless you speak of your own knowledge.''

Jean seemed on the point of making some remark, but checked himself and shrugged his shoulders again and held his peace.

'' But if he is dead, what has become of Madge Linwood, who went away in his canoe with him ? '' asked the distracted Asher Norris.

The answer of the Canadian was another shrug of the shoulders. If he possessed knowledge of the missing one—and Asher believed that he did possess such knowledge—he was holding it back. The impatient young man felt like throttling him and forcing the secret from his lips, but prudence forbade.

Standing in the dim light of the moon, Asher noted something peculiar in the action and manner of Jean. Naturally the two faced each other, but Jean, while often looking into his face, kept glancing across in the direction of the fringe of wood and undergrowth that lined the river, as if something in that direction specially interested him. Asher also turned his head, and caught the dim outline of a man's figure, standing as motionless as a statue, evidently with his attention fixed upon the American and Canadian.

" Who is he ? " asked Asher, in an undertone.

Without inquiring as to whom was meant, Jean Chotean answered:

" He is Jacques Faire, a neighbor."

The man was too faintly shown for young Norris to make sure whether this was the truth, but he suspected that instead of a Canadian the other was an Indian, whose keen vision had roused a suspicion of Asher's identity, if indeed he had not already learned that he was an American from the other side of the river.

Jean spoke with sudden excitement:

" You are in greater danger than you think; you

have waited too long, my friend Asher; you cannot escape from the settlement.''

" I would like to know who will hinder me,'' demanded the youth, his combative nature fully roused.

" The Ottawas have found out that you are here; if you try to leave they will make you prisoner; you know what that means.''

" But I am not a prisoner yet !''

He was about to move away, when Jean seized his arm.

" Come with me ; don't hesitate ; don't look around; walk fast, or you are lost.''

Before the youth had time to collect his thoughts he was walking rapidly, his guide still holding his arm with nervous grip. They passed in front of Pierre Muire's house, and still following the winding path which answered for a street, left three other cabins behind them, when the guide abruptly turned to the left, stepped upon a low wooden porch and shoved open a door, into which he pushed Asher, with himself closely behind him.

The room which they had entered was similar to the main apartment of most of the houses in the Canadian settlement. It occupied the whole lower floor, which was the living room of the house. There were a table, a few wooden chairs, several cheap pictures on the walls, scant furniture, and a fire burning on the hearth. With the door closed and the sultry night, the air inside was insufferably close.

The only occupant of this room, when the two hurriedly entered, was the wife of Jean Chotean, a plain, coarse woman in middle life. She was in the act of crossing the apartment to attend to some household duty, when she halted and turned wonderingly toward the two. Her husband said something in French by way of explanation. Asher, who had an imperfect knowledge of the tongue, did not catch its meaning, but it seemed to satisfy the woman, who nodded her head, turned slowly to the nearest chair, deliberately sat down and folded her hands in her lap, like a pattern of the meek, submissive wife.

Meantime, Jean Chotean was not idle. Turning about, he deftly drew in the latch string. While this locked the cumbrous door, he was not satisfied. The heavy wooden bar was lifted from where it leaned against the log wall and slipped into place across the door, which was now secured so firmly that nothing less than a battering ram was sufficient to drive it inward.

Hardly was this done, when some one on the outside struck the door several resounding knocks, though no words were spoken.

The reflection of the firelight on the face of the

Canadian showed that he was scared, and for the
moment " rattled." He glanced hurriedly around,
as if seeking some way out of a bad dilemma.
Asher Norris, believing they were about to be
attacked, grasped his rifle more firmly, and pointed
to where Jean's weapon was suspended on a couple
of deer's antlers over the fireplace.

" You take your gun, Jean, and we 'll fight them
all."

" No, no, no!" replied the host, more agitated
than ever; " it will be the death of us both. Run
up there ! "

He pointed to the sloping ladder which led to the
upper story, and Asher, who from the singular turn
that matters had taken was unable to think clearly,
ran nimbly up the ladder into the dim room above.

The next moment he felt that he had done a foolish thing, equivalent to stepping into the mouth of
a pit yawning before him. Had he remained on the
lower floor he would have been able to make a
staunch fight, with the chance of reaching the outside at some favorable moment, but now all such
hope was gone.

His familiarity with the construction of the Canadian houses told him that there were two apart-
ments above stairs, mainly used at night. Each
was lighted by two small windows, which were so
narrow that no man could force his body through

them. It was the same with the windows on the lower floor, such being the custom of pioneers, who meant the openings to serve for light and for port-holes, but never to admit an enemy.

The top of the ladder projected a couple of feet above the upper level. Asher stepped out upon the rough, puncheon floor, but made no attempt at investigation. He was too much interested in what was occurring below. Standing close to the open-ing, he listened.

The vigorous knocking was renewed. Indeed it had not ceased, and the man or men on the outside were losing patience. An angry voice demanded admittance, and Jean Chotean, as if frightened out of his senses, now unbarred the door. The next moment the visitor stepped inside.

As he did so he spoke, and one sound of his voice was sufficient for Asher Norris to identify him as an Ottawa Indian.

CHAPTER XII.

ON THE RIVER'S MARGIN.

TO Asher Norris, standing at the head of the ladder, there was but one explanation of these singular incidents.

Despite the declaration of Jean Chotean, the Frenchman, there could be no doubt that while the two were talking in front of the house of Pierre Muire, they had attracted the notice of one of the hostiles prowling through the settlement. With his finely trained faculties he identified the man conversing with the Canadian, and with the hatred of his leader Pontiac determined to encompass his death.

It was charitable to believe that Jean wished to save the American, though it was also possible that his warning was meant to start him at once on his flight, so that the Canadian might get the matter off his hands, and leave to others the settlement of the question of life and death.

But his subsequent action agreed with the theory that the man really wished to save the youth. Hoping that the eavesdropper had not identified him, Jean hurried to his own home and locked Asher within, leaving the question of his final escape from the settlement to be determined by events as they came up.

But hardly had the two entered, when the Indian knocked and demanded admittance. On the supposition that there was but one of them, the obvious course for Jean would have been to admit him without delay. Asher Norris held no single warrior in fear, and, leaving the Canadian to act a neutral part, Asher could have disposed of him with little delay and then gone forth from the cabin unquestioned.

But such an incident would have involved the host in the gravest trouble. The death of the warrior would have been investigated and the Canadian's life endangered, if not forfeited. It was unreasonable to expect him to consent to anything of that nature, losing sight of the fact that he was so agitated that he was uncertain of the right course to follow.

All this was disquieting enough, but the youth crouching at the top of the ladder was tormented by another suspicion, amounting to a belief, that Jean Chotean had aimed to play him false from the beginning. When he first warned him to flee, he may have been honest, but from the moment he discovered that the two were under the surveillance of an Ottawa warrior, every point played was with a view of Asher Norris's betrayal.

The latter listened intently in the oppressive stillness. The wife was evidently sitting in her chair, and taking no part in the conversation, but Jean and the Ottawa talked earnestly and in low tones. The Canadian understood the Indian lingo which was employed, so that when the listener now and then caught a word, he could form no idea of its meaning. That the dusky miscreant knew of the American's presence in the house was self-evident; the two were evidently discussing the best way of disposing of him.

" They will hardly dare to venture up the ladder to attack me; I wish they would."

Suddenly the talking ceased. Asher listened with the same closeness as before, but it was not renewed. What could it mean ?

Actuated by his great fear, the youth knelt down softly until he was able to lower his head, so as to see into the room. To his amazement neither Chotean nor the Ottawa was visible. The wife sat in her chair with folded hands, as if she had not stirred from the moment she took her seat, but she was the only occupant of the lower floor.

Despite the attention with which Asher Norris had listened, the two men had opened, passed out, and closed the door without his hearing them. It seemed incredible, but it was the fact.

" They have gone to bring help; a party of them

8

will be back in a few minutes, and then I shall be like a rat in a trap—that is if I wait, which I shall not do.''

Placing his foot on a round of the ladder he descended as nimbly as he had climbed the primitive stairs a few minutes before. The instant the woman saw him coming down, she rose in a startled way from her chair, and, holding up her hands, exclaimed:

'' Go back ! go back ! you must stay till they return!''

She did not speak English as well as her husband, but her words were unmistakable. Uttered in her excitement, they confirmed the fears that had moved the young man to action.

'' I am going to leave this house,'' he said, pausing for an instant in the middle of the floor.

'' You must not! you must stay! They will soon be back ! If they find you are not here, they will kill Jean and me !''

She interposed as if to keep him from reaching the door. The eyes of Asher Norris flashed. Clubbing his rifle, he said in a voice low of deadly meaning:

'' Stand aside, or I will strike you to the floor!''

Frightened by his terrible looks and manner, she threw up her hands, as if to ward off the impending blow, and retreating to her chair dropped into it with a collapse that must have threatened the structure.

"GO BACK! GO BACK!"

She had done all she could to restrain the captive, and now simply stared at him, without movement or word.

Not a second was to spare. The heavy wooden bar was leaning against the side of the house and the door was held only by the latch, whose string was still inside, Jean not having taken the time to run the end through the small orifice. When he should return, his knock would cause the door's instant opening by the waiting wife.

Asher Norris raised the latch, stepped outside and drew the door shut. His fear was that the woman would make an outcry that would bring her husband and the Indians to the spot, but she was too terrified to think of that.

The youth stood still for a moment, looking and listening. To the right could be seen the glow of the wood fires shining through the front doors and windows of the cabins strung in that direction, while to the left the same was observed. He saw no one moving about, for the hour had become late.

Crouching low, to conceal himself as far as possible, Asher ran across the space intervening between him and the fringe of wood on the bank of the river. The distance was slight, and he held his breath until among the friendly shadows. Then kneeling, he listened and watched.

His flight was not a moment too soon, for hardly

had he reached his concealment when the familiar guttural exclamation was heard from a point toward the upper end of the settlement. At the same moment he made out the figures of four men approaching at a rapid pace, the foremost of whom he recognized in the moonlight as Jean Chotean, the others being Indians, fully armed.

It was marvellous how quickly these miscreants had been brought to the scene, but the whole thing was clear to Norris. Finding himself detected, the Canadian had made it appear that he had inveigled the American into his house for the purpose of entrapping him (and Asher believed such to be the fact), after which he and the Ottawa had gone for help in making the youth a prisoner.

The latter waited where he was until the four stopped at the door, and, after a moment's delay, were admitted. Then, feeling that his situation was too dangerous to be held, he began stealing along the bank and away from the dreaded spot. His flight must be discovered within a few seconds, and the Ottawas would neglect no chance of securing him before he could get beyond their reach.

The task of the young man was a difficult one, for he was likely to betray himself by the rustling of the bushes and the breaking of twigs under his feet, but as yet no one was hunting for him, and special care was not necessary.

The temptation to enter the river and swim for the other side was strong, though he was handicapped by his rifle, which he could not well secure to his back, but he decided not to resort to that until no other way was left open to him.

The point where he had left his canoe was not far, and his familiarity with the settlement enabled him to reach the spot with no loss of time. But there he was met by a surprise and disappointment: his canoe was gone.

Under other circumstances he would have explained this as a mistake on his part as to the spot, but his certainty could not have been greater had the sun been shining in the sky.

" Since some one has taken my boat I shall have to take the boat of some one," was the philosophical conclusion of the youth, who lost no time in searching for that which was lost. He continued stealing up the bank of the river, knowing that he would not have to go far before coming upon one of the numerous canoes that were always strung along the shore.

He heard nothing of his pursuers, but an Indian when hunting for a foe does not do so with a brass band, and they might be at that moment within a few rods of him. His care, therefore, was so great that his progress was slow.

Good fortune attended him, for he had gone

scarcely fifty feet, when his outstretched hand touched the side of one of the bark structures lying across his path and close to the edge of the water. Lifting it carefully from the ground, he carried it a few paces and then set it down so gently in the current that hardly a ripple was produced.

" It weighs about the same as mine, and, by gracious! It is mine!"

Such was the fact. Despite the obscurity he recognized the craft as the one in which he had crossed the river earlier in the evening, and to which he was as much accustomed as to his own rifle. It was hard to account for its removal from where he had left it, but the fact was a warning that he did not forget. Whoever had transferred it must expect to return, and perhaps at that time was on his way. Possibly it was Jean Chotean or one of the Ottawas.

It was this fear that led Asher to seat himself in the craft and drive it fully a hundred yards up stream, before venturing to halt. Then, feeling that none of his enemies would know where to look for him, he checked the boat, holding it motionless by seizing one of the overhanging limbs.

The trouble was that just then the sky had become so freed of drifting clouds that the moon shone with unobstructed light, which was so reflected from the unruffled surface of the river that he dared not venture into it,

" And why should I leave this shore ? "

This was the question that he asked himself before
he again laid hand on his canoe. He had set out to
search for Madge Linwood, of whose whereabouts
he had not gained the first idea. She might be
somewhere on the eastern shore, and still in the
French settlement. At any rate, if Asher Norris
went back to the fort, the most that he could say
was that Pierre Muire had started to take her home
more than twenty-four hours before, since which
time nothing was known of either. The knight
errant, therefore, would be confessing that he was
able to do naught toward clearing up the mystery,
and such confession he would not make while life
remained.

His brain was in a state of turmoil, for he was sure
that never had any person been confronted by so
puzzling a problem. Convinced that Jean Chotean
was able to tell him far more than he had told, he
was still powerless to use that source of information.
It would not do for him again to meet the Canadian
that had tried to betray him into the hands of the
Ottawas, for, aside from the resentment he felt
toward the man, no reliance could be placed upon
his words.

Asher Norris asked himself whether there was
not some one in the settlement who had an inkling
of the truth, and who could be trusted to make

it known. He knew nearly every settler, and he called to mind a number whose word was worthy of belief, but it was a staggering problem as to how he could open communication with them, at the very time that a party of Ottawas were searching the place for him.

"Ah, if Uncle Jo were here," was the thought that would obtrude itself, despite its idleness, "but he is n't, nor will he be for days to come, and within that time the fate of poor Madge must be set-tled——"

Sitting thus in the canoe, with one hand gently grasping a tiny limb and his senses keyed to the highest point, he became aware that he was not alone. Some person was moving along the bank, close to the water's edge.

"It 's one of the Ottawas," was the conclusion of Asher Norris, but he was mistaken.

CHAPTER XIII.

CATHARINE.

SEATED in the small canoe, held perfectly motionless, Asher Norris had nothing to do but to listen. He was far enough under the overhanging bushes to be wrapped in shadow, so that no change of position could help him.

How could any person, be he ever so subtle and skilled in woodcraft, learn where he was in hiding, when there was absolutely nothing to guide such person ? And yet, as if there is really a sixth sense, this very thing was done.

Confident that the man, if hunting for him, would pass beyond, the youth listened to his movements, which were readily traced in the perfect stillness, for the current was so sluggish thus close to shore that it made no ripple against the prow of the light canoe. Furthermore, the individual groping along the land did not seem to take pains to veil his movements.

Asher heard him draw the bushes aside, after which the moccasined foot was pressed upon the yielding ground. Then the hands parted the undergrowth again and the careful step was repeated.

121

When first detected the stranger was nearer the settlement than the American, and several minutes passed before he reached a point opposite the canoe. Then he went two or three paces beyond.

" He will keep that up till he grows tired, and then conclude——"

Could Asher Norris credit his senses ?   The other had paused as if aware that he had gone too far, and it was necessary to retrace his steps.   How in the name of the seven wonders had he learned the fact ?   The youth had heard his uncle tell of such things, but he had never before experienced anything of the kind, nor did he believe it possible until this moment.

Back, step by step, for three paces, which was slightly too far, and then there was a second pause. Wonderful to relate, the stranger had discovered that he was once more beyond soundings.   So he halted, stood still a moment, retrograded for one pace, and then came to a final stop.   He had struck the right spot and knew it.

" That 's as near a miracle as anything comes in this world," thought Asher Norris with a feeling of awe.

Pausing only a few seconds, the stranger began moving once more through the wood and undergrowth, but now he was coming toward the canoe. The situation of Asher Norris was critical.   If he remained where he was the warrior would be able to shoot or to hurl his tomahawk with unerring aim, and being in deeper concealment could not be detected.

Asher was about to let go of the straining limb, so as to float with the sluggish current, when the other spoke:

" Is that my brother ? "

If a ghost had addressed the young man he could not have been more startled than by these words. It was not a white man, nor an Indian warrior that had thus spoken, but Catharine, the Ojibwa girl that had given Major Gladwyn warning of the plan of Pontiac to massacre the garrison. It was she who in searching for Asher had given so marvellous a display of woodcraft.

The youth drove his canoe against the shore at the feet of the girl, who seemed to expect something of that nature. The gloom was so deep that neither could see the other, but had they chosen they might have clasped hands, and their voices were so modu-lated that Pontiac himself, if within two or three yards, would not have heard them.

" Catharine, I am glad you have come, but how did you know where I was ? "

She spoke English as if to the manner born.

" I saw my brother leave the house of Jean Chotean."

" Did you see me go in ? "

" You and he went in; he and Gray Wolf came out together; they had gone for other warriors to slay my brother; then you came forth and hurried away; had you waited but a little while, you would have been too late."

" You are right as to that, for I saw the four returning and knew they expected to get my scalp. Did you remove my canoe from where I left it to this place ? "

" No ; Catharine knew nothing of that ; she looked for you; for she had something to tell you that your heart yearns to know."

Asher would have insisted upon her explaining how she succeeded in locating him in the remarkable manner described, but for these last words which set his heart a-throbbing with hope and fear.

" Have you something to tell me of Madge Linwood ? "

" I have something to tell you of her; I saw her when she came to the home of the sick woman; Pierre Muire brought her there; that never should have been."

" It would not had I been at the fort, but I was away."

" My brother does not understand what Catharine means."

" You mean that Madge went into great danger,

when she came to the settlement, for that is proved because she is missing.''

'' It is not that which I mean, but Pierre Muire loves the white maiden; he wished to make her his wife, as the white people call their squaws.''

These words went through Asher Norris like a knife-thrust. It was not idle suspicion, then, on his part, for this wise Indian maiden had noted it. Pierre was in love with Madge, even though his mother was at the point of death and may have asked for her. Probably it was that fact which prompted the action to the young man.

'' But Pierre set out last night to take her home, as he promised.''

'' And yet he did not get there.''

'' Not unless he returned this evening.''

'' He has not returned; he will never return. But Pierre was not the only one who loves the beautiful maiden.''

Asher blushed in the darkness, for he supposed she referred to him, but he was dumfounded the next moment by the declaration:

'' Pontiac, the great chieftain of the Ottawas, loves her for whom the heart of my brother yearns.''

'' Heavens! can it be possible ? I never dreamed of that!''

'' Pontiac loves the pale-faced maiden !''

" The wretch! he has a wife; what business has he to look upon Madge Linwood ? "

Catharine was silent, as if the question was beyond her power of reply.   It struck Asher Norris that this was an unprecedented state of affairs. Here was Madge, not yet out of her girlhood, looked upon with covetous eyes by him, an American; by Pierre Muire, a French Canadian ; and Pontiac, the Ottawa chieftain.   It would seem as if some other nationality ought to be represented among the claimants for her hand.

" Pierre started last night to take Madge home. Did you see them depart ? "

" Catharine stood on the shore and waved good-by to her friend.   She sat at the front of the canoe, and Pierre used the paddle.   They headed across the river, and by and by the darkness shut them out from sight.   Catharine saw them no more.   Pierre has not come back, and the pale-faced maiden is not at home."

" How came you to know that, Catharine ? "

" My brother said so to Jean Chotean."

" And you overheard us!   You are a wonderful girl.   But can you tell me where Madge is ? "

" Only the Great Spirit knows, but Catharine thinks she is with Pontiac."

" Then where is Pierre ? "

" Dead."

" I do not understand how that can be. Pontiac was the friend of Pierre."

" But when he finds that Pierre loves the maiden, then Pierre is his enemy."

" But last night Pontiac was with his warriors nine or ten miles from here. I know it, for I was on the schooner which the Indians attacked far down the river, and I saw Pontiac with my own eyes."

" But Pontiac could travel many miles since then; some of his warriors may have brought the maiden to him."

" Well," said Asher, " this is beyond my ken. Catharine, you can find out where Madge is. If you will do so it will make the hearts of her friends glad."

" Catharine will try."

He was about to repeat his urging, when he discovered that she was with him no longer. He heard a slight rustling, and, without a parting word, she vanished.

Perhaps it was as well, since she had no more to tell him, nor would he have been likely to accept advice from her, much as he admired her wonderful woodcraft.

He had learned that Pierre Muire had set out on the previous evening with Madge Linwood in his canoe, and had headed for Fort Detroit. Thus far everything coincided with his promises and with his statements.   His mother was mortally ill, and, despite that fact, he had left her to return the girl to her parents, as he had pledged to do when he took her away.   Scrutinized up to this point, his conduct was straightforward and honorable.

But the momentous question remained as to what had become of the two, after passing out upon the river in the darkness of night.   When beyond reach of all prying eyes, the young man may have carried out an intention previously formed.   Forgetting his stricken parent in his infatuation for the girl, perhaps he took her to some point where he expected to make her confess her love and promise to become his wife ere she could return to her home.

But the intrusion of Pontiac into the affair seemed to twist all theories askew.   With the almost unlimited power possessed by the chieftain at that time, there was little hope of thwarting his imperious will.   He had so many to do his bidding that, though he may have been miles from the scene of action, some of his warriors would have seized the chance to serve him.

It was impossible for the sorely troubled Asher to remain idle while these and hundreds of similar thoughts were seething through his brain.   Catharine being gone, he pushed the canoe from shore, just far enough off to allow it to clear the overhanging vegetation, when he began paddling slowly and silently down stream in the direction of the fort, or rather parallel with that direction, since he did not venture out into the channel.

This was what might be considered the " back trail," since it carried him in front of the settle- ment, and past the home of Jean Chotean, from which he had escaped just in time to save his life. He needed no one to remind him of the need of care, though it was to be supposed that the friends of Chotean had finished their search of the immedi- ate neighborhood of his house, and were now look- ing elsewhere.

And so it was that he drifted downward, some- times using his paddle, listening intently and con- tinually glancing about him. The sky remained quite clear, so that the moon shone without ob- struction, and he was able to see for a considerable distance over the calmly flowing river.

He was not mistaken, therefore, when just on the farthest line of vision, he traced the outlines of a canoe, floating with the current. It went faster than he would have gone, had he not used his pad- dle, since the current was more rapid than near shore. The boat drifted with the silence of a shadow, and, urged by a curiosity which prudence would have told him to restrain, Asher paddled a slight way from the protecting gloom that he might

9

gain a closer view.   He remained so near the shore that in the event of danger he could dart among the vegetation and leap out upon land.

There was a single person in the other boat.   He was sitting near the stern, or rather the rear, since both ends were the same, with drooping head and idle arms.   So far as the youth could make out, he held no paddle, but appeared like a man asleep.

Mindful of the clever tricks to which the American Indian resorts to deceive his enemy, Asher advanced with extreme caution, but something familiar in the appearance of the other led him to dip his paddle more deeply and to forget the danger behind him.

Thus approaching, the American suddenly uttered an exclamation of astonishment.   He had recognized the man, and swept his boat alongside, calling out to him in an incautiously loud voice.

There was no movement or anything in the nature of a response.   Nor indeed could there be, for Pierre Muire, who sat with bowed head and motionless arms, was dead.

THE LAST OF PIERRE.

CHAPTER XIV.

A CANOE AND ITS OCCUPANT.

IT was a terrifying discovery, and, accustomed as Asher Norris had become to scenes of violence, he never was more deeply impressed than by the sight of the lifeless body of Pierre Muire, sitting with drooping head and arms, at the stern of the canoe, which was drifting down the Detroit river.

His next thought was of her that had been his passenger, and, scarcely breathing, he leaned over and peered into the boat. Thank God, it was empty!

Empty not of her alone, but of everything except the body of the hapless French Canadian. Placing his hand upon the face he found it cold. Doubtless the poor fellow had been dead for many hours. If stricken while paddling, the oar had slipped from his hand and floated off. His legs were outstretched in front of him, and his position would have been natural to any man that had given way to drowsiness and was sleeping soundly.

There was enough moonlight for Asher to see the point where the bullet had entered the left breast,

bringing death as suddenly as if from the lightning
bolt.   Unfortunate Pierre Muire!   A brief while
before he was the embodiment of physical strength
and vigor, and now he had gone to join his widowed
mother, or perhaps he had preceded her into the
mysterious land of shadows.

The heart of Asher Norris smote him, for he was
convinced now that he had done the dead man a
great injustice.   He may have loved Madge—doubtless he did—but who could be blamed for that ?
But he had meant to keep his pledge to her parents,
and, whether or not he declared his love, he intended
to deliver her unharmed to them.   And while striving to do so he had been laid low by some one.

" Killed by an Indian, that thereby he might
please Pontiac," was the thought of the young
man, whose anger was kindled against the terrible
Ottawa; " they slew Pierre and took away Madge."

This conclusion would have seemed reasonable,
but for the fact that more than twenty-four hours
had passed since the Canadian left his home with
Madge Linwood.   Where had the two been in
the interval, and how came it that, on the second
night, the body of Pierre was found floating down
the river in his canoe, near the spot where the crime
must have been committed ?

It was too late to atone for the unjust suspicion
held toward his old acquaintance, but a chivalrous

impulse led Asher to do that which might be considered his last tribute, and which was attended with great personal risk to himself.

In guiding his boat down stream he had approached the southern termination of the settlement, and was somewhat below the former home of Pierre. He could make no mistake as to the spot. With a thong from his buckskin breeches he fastened the other canoe to his own, and paddled silently to the place from which he fled in such affright but a brief while before. It was now fully midnight, and few of the people were astir. He did not aim for a spot above or below the house where the watchers were with the dead body, but, striking the point with almost mathematical exactness, he stepped out and drew the second boat far up the bank, where it could not be swept away by the action of the current.

" Some one will find it to-morrow and give it decent burial beside the body of his mother. Pity that Pontiac and all his crew could not pass out of existence at the same time ! "

This duty done, Asher again entered his canoe, as much at a loss as to what he should do as after hearing the story of Catharine, the Ojibwa maiden. He was paddling back and forth, going hither and thither, gaining slight information, but securing nothing that could give the desired clew, and with-

out any knowledge of where he should look for her
who was dearer than all the world to him.

But hold! Was he really so destitute of information? Catharine believed that Madge Linwood was
in the Ottawa village, a prisoner of Pontiac, and the
incident just described conformed to such belief.
It looked as if Pierre had been shot while in mid-
stream by some follower of the chieftain who knew
of his infatuation for the girl, and that she had been
taken out of the boat, while her protector was left
to himself.

The canoe may have been near shore when the
fatal shot was fired, or perhaps it was accidentally
caught in some obstruction which held it until
it loosened in the same manner to drift down
stream. The cause of the delay was thus readily
explained.

If the missing one was in the Ottawa village, the
difficulty of rescuing her looked very great. Pontiac had so many warriors on both sides of the
river, with others joining him, that Major Gladwyn
had no power to force him to do anything. The
garrison, as we have learned, was so weak that the
most the commandant could hope to do was to
stand off the chieftain and his savages who were
besieging him until through weariness they would
give up the task. If any illustration were needed
of the folly of attacking the hostiles, it had already

been furnished in the frightful repulse of Major Dalzell at Bloody Ridge.

There had been some exchanges of prisoners with Pontiac, but they were few. It need not be said that if the leader had formed a fancy for Madge Linwood and had succeeded in securing possession of her, Major Gladwyn could not capture enough Indians to give in exchange for her.

All this being so, where could there be any hope of saving Madge ? It would seem that there was little indeed. But youth, vigor, and naturally bounding spirits cannot long remain cast down, and, dark as the situation looked, Asher Norris did not yield to despair.

There were three grounds upon which he based his hope: In the first place, Madge Linwood was bright and brave and daring, and she might be able to help herself. She knew the nature of the people that had made her captive, and possibly would find a way of turning that knowledge to account. Again, the interest of Catharine, the Ojibwa girl, had been enlisted. She was one of the most cunning of her race. While she carried the momentous secret of Pontiac's plan for the massacre of the garrison to Major Gladwyn, as well as other hardly less important matters, that chieftain, with all his shrewdness, never held any suspicion of her. Had he known the truth he would have sunk his tomahawk into her brain with the suddenness of the lightning stroke.

Finally Pontiac had set his heart upon capturing Detroit. He knew that some of the posts, like · Mackinaw, Le Bœuf, and others had fallen, and he had promised the different tribes that the leading fort of all should be burned to ashes and the garrison given to the tomahawk, and that his hand should kindle the blaze.

Pontiac, as is known, ranks among the great Indians of history, with an ambition as towering as that of King Philip or Tecumseh. He would use all the means possible to bring about the success of his gigantic conspiracy, for with him he would gain or lose all ; and while his infatuation for a young woman of the hated race was as unabated as ever, the realization of the dream of his life must necessarily employ much of his thoughts and energies. Such being the fact, the wisdom of the Ojibwa maiden and of Madge Linwood would find some scope.

The one objectionable feature in all this was that it necessarily eliminated Asher Norris from the problem. The part he was to play was no part at all, beyond that of spectator, and it was impossible for him to consent to this.

The temptation was strong to venture near the encampment of the Ottawas, with a hope of gaining more definite knowledge, and possibly of communicating with the girl. How that was to be brought about, even he, with his naturally buoyant spirits, was unable to figure out.

While these thoughts were following one another through his brain, he acted upon a sudden resolution of returning to Detroit with the news already obtained. It was remotely possible, too, that tidings had reached the post that might be of service to him.

Accordingly, his canoe was headed toward the western bank, and he sent it swiftly over the moonlit surface, fearing no pursuit, though the prowling Indians were on every side of the post. It was well beyond midnight when his boat touched land, and he stepped out. He was in peril from the hostiles, who, like birds of the night, were always prowling in the vicinity, on the watch for some chance of doing harm to the place that had defied their efforts for months. By care, he succeeded in reaching the gate without molestation, and, making himself known, was admitted by the sentinels.

He made his way straight to his own home, where the latch-string was hanging out, though both of his parents had been asleep for hours. He entered softly, and climbing to his room, retired to rest, not waking until the sun was shining. When he descended, his mother was surprised and delighted.

His father was absent, but returned while the son was partaking of his morning meal.

His story was quickly told, and in reply to his inquiries, he was informed that, so far as his parents knew, nothing further had been heard of Madge Linwood, though it was possible some news had arrived late at night.

Asher's next act was to visit the stricken parents of the girl, who listened with painful interest to what he told them.

"Poor Pierre!" said the father; "he was killed while doing his duty, but many others have fallen by the hands of these miscreants, as many more must fall before they are driven into the forests where they belong."

"Surely Pontiac will use one so young and innocent with mercy," said the mother, who, like her husband, held no thought of the real reason why the chieftain had made her captive, for Asher did not deem it well to harrow their feelings by revealing the whole truth.

"He has never been accused of being a merciful Indian," said he; "but I have a hope that he will not use her ill, because if such was his intention he hardly would have taken the trouble to make her prisoner."

"Perhaps the Ojibwa girl will find some way of befriending her, for the two loved each other; but,

Asher, it is clear that there is nothing further for you to do."

" I am sure you will be content now to remain at home," added the husband; " for you cannot expect Pontiac to treat you with consideration when you fall into his hands."

" As yet I have not fallen into his hands," was the response of the youth.

" For which you are to be congratulated, and for which, too, I am sure you are grateful, but when you cannot be of any help to Madge, you are too considerate to add to the grief of your parents and friends by causing them to mourn your death."

Asher was annoyed by the way in which these good people looked at the matter. He thought that if his own parents could urge him to assume every risk for the sake of the missing one, surely her parents ought to be mute. But he withheld explaining his purpose, and, bidding them good-by, he took his departure.

Earlier that evening than before, he stole away from the post and returned to the spot where he had left his canoe. It was found undisturbed, and entering the craft he sent it skimming up stream. He did not hug the shore as closely as before, for the necessity was absent. The sky had clouded during the afternoon, and a fog enveloped wood and river, with rain impending. He was relieved that such was the fact, though it promised to add to his discomfort, for it would be hard to find shelter from the dampness; but it removed the need of extreme caution used on the previous night. He could paddle swiftly without peering on every hand for enemies, though there remained the possibility of coming unawares upon a whole boat-load of hostiles.

Now and then he held his paddle suspended and listened, but aware as he was that the redmen could drive a canoe as noiselessly as he, he was too wise to feel fully secure. But during the day he had formulated his plan of action, and was now vigorously following it out with the resolve to push it to the speediest conclusion possible.

CHAPTER XV.

ASHER NORRIS had decided upon his course of action after long deliberation — a fact which in no way lessened its foolhardiness. It was, in brief, to make his way to the immediate vicinity of the Ottawa village and learn, if possible, not only whether Madge Linwood was there, but whether he could not do something to aid in securing her release from captivity and return to her people.

Had the young man been asked to explain how all this was to be brought about, he would have been unable to answer, but his affection for the distressed one, his youth, daring, and high spirits fanned the belief that some way would open to carry out the scheme that was so dear to his heart.

He accepted the damp, foggy night as an omen of good fortune. Persons of his temperament are inclined to see favorable omens where none exist, wrongly interpreting them until they awake too late from their error. Since in the night he resembled in looks and appearance the Canadians, who were friendly to the Indians, he was hopeful of being mistaken for one of them, his great drawback being that he was unable to speak the patois used by those people.

Since it would have involved a long, circuitous course to pass around the upper or lower end of the settlement, he meant to walk directly through it. If the Ottawas saw him coming from that direction, they would be more likely to take him for one of the settlers than if he approached from another point of the compass. While he was well known to all the white men, it was not to be expected that the hostiles would recognize him, unless brought face to face with them. It was his English converse with Jean Chotean, within the hearing of Gray Wolf, which awoke the suspicion of the latter, and came so near bringing about his own downfall.

Advancing diagonally across the river, the youth had passed about half the distance, when his keen sense of hearing told him he was near some other boat that was approaching. He ceased paddling and listened. The almost inaudible ripple and swish of oars showed that the other craft was between him and the eastern shore, and was coming in a line that would bring it close to him.

" They may be Ottawas or Canadians," was his reflection, as he drove his own boat farther up stream; " but whichever they are, it is as well that we should not meet."

Despite his closeness of attention, he quickly discovered that he had made a mistake, or the others
had changed their course, for, when he again held
his paddle motionless, the stranger was heard almost
upon him. Impatient that this should be the fact,
he again swung the suspended paddle, but before
the craft yielded to the impulse, a large canoe containing eight or nine persons, loomed out of the fog
and darkness, so near and heading so directly
toward him, that he would have been run down, had
he not abruptly sheered his craft to the left. Instantly one of the men called in English:

"This is no time to be abroad! You are in
danger."

"From whom?" asked Asher, still shying off
from the Canadians, for he suspected that among
the party were several Indians.

"From Pontiac and his warriors. A good many
are on the river to-night."

"And why more to-night than any other time?"

"You must ask him," replied the other, with
something like a chortle, as if pleased with the
situation.

"Neither Major Gladwyn nor any of us fears Pontiac and all the imps he can bring together."

"Boast not, Asher," added the other, recognizing his voice, "for you will be surprised in a few
days. Take the advice of a friend and get back to

the post while you have the chance, for it will not be yours for long."

" I thank you for your words, and will be on my guard."

While this brief conversation was going on, Asher continued to edge away from the larger boat, for he was suspicious. It, too, was moving off, and the words given were the last that were exchanged. Immediately the two craft lost sight of each other.

But there was food for reflection in the words of the Canadian, whom the youth did not identify, though his voice had a familiar sound. The Ottawa chieftain was a restless leader, who could not be content to sit down with his warriors in front of Detroit and wait for the garrison to yield through starvation. The hostiles had kept up a pestering fire from the outbuildings, as has been shown, until dislodged by the hot shot which burned the structures ; they had assailed and overwhelmed Major Dalzell and his command ; had attempted to destroy the two schooners by means of fire rafts, and whenever one of those vessels passed up or down the river, it was running a gauntlet between the Indian encampments on the shores of the stream. While it would seem that the chieftain must be near the end of his resources, yet he held no such belief, for the besieging forces were continually increased by the arrival of warriors, some of them from a long distance. All were in buoyant spirits, bringing as they did news of the fall of more than one western post, and confident that Detroit would soon be added to the dismal list of victims to Indian treachery and cunning.

Pontiac's fiery speeches to these reinforcements showed that his hopes were higher than at any time since the failure of his plan to surprise Major Gladwyn. It would seem, therefore, likely that there was wisdom in the warning of the Canadian, who advised Asher to turn back while he had the chance to do so. All this might be true, indeed; nevertheless, his counsel was wasted on the young man, who, hardly waiting until they were hidden from sight, renewed his paddling toward the eastern bank.

The fog had now become a cold drizzle, which soon saturated his garments. It would be hard to imagine a more uncomfortable night, but the men who lived on the frontier were too inured to hardship to care for a trifle like that. The moisture covered his face and hands, trickled from his hair and seemed to soak through everything with which it came in contact, but he continued to sway his paddle, as if the moon were shining from an unclouded sky.

He would have been unpardonably careless had he wholly disregarded the words of his friend. He did not doubt that many hostiles were on the river,

10

and it was not unlikely that a large number of them were crossing to the western shore with some new plan of attack in view. He, therefore, propelled his boat with unusual care, ceasing after every few strokes, and listening with close attention. He had a habit of flitting his head from side to side with a bird-like quickness, so as to make sure that if any suspicious noise was heard, he learned the point of the compass whence it came.

It was because of this extreme caution that he had gone only a little way when he made the unpleasant discovery that another canoe was immediately in front of him. Uncertain as to its course, he ceased paddling, bent his head and intently listened.

To his surprise, at the moment of doing so, the sound of paddling stopped, as if those in the other boat were doing the same as himself. Could it be that, despite his extreme care, they had been equally quick to detect his presence ? It appeared hardly possible, but he was wise enough to act upon the theory. He moved the paddle with a stealth that prevented all betrayal, heading now directly up stream, and not pausing until he had passed several rods.

Still he failed to hear anything, but once he caught something in the nature of a gentle ripple from the direction of the first sound. One thing had become evident: he was now dealing with past masters in woodcraft. He was doubtless near a party of Indians who knew how to approach a foe or intended victim without betraying themselves. Unexpectedly he had run into peril, when he had no thought of it, and it would require his utmost skill to prevent a disastrous failure when on the very threshold of his enterprise.

Asher resolved that if discovered he would run his boat at all speed against the eastern bank, which was nearer than the western shore, leap out and take to the woods, where he was confident of eluding a score of enemies.

Suddenly a section of the fog near the surface of the river seemed to become denser. While he wondered what it meant, he saw uncouth figures with swaying arms, growing momentarily more distinct, until he resolved them into men who were guiding their canoe toward him. The occupants had located him and were near at hand.

The other craft, which was fully as large as the Canadian one, contained as many persons, and was approaching from down the river, so that it was as easy to speed to one side as to the other. Instead of doing so, however, the youth dipped his paddle deep and plied it with all the power at his command. It shot forward, like the flight of a swallow, for there was no more skilful canoeist than Asher Norris.

No sound came from the pursuer, whose occupants at once bent their energies to the task of overtaking him. It was a fair chase, and only a few minutes were needed to decide who was to be the winner.

Fearful of failure, the fugitive sheered his boat toward the bank, so that, if worst came to worst, he would have the wooded shore for a final refuge, but before that came into view the thrilling fact became apparent that he could travel faster than the others. The dim figures and the boat gradually grew indistinct, and soon faded from sight, though the paddles were .swung with the same tremendous vigor as if the Indians expected to tire out the white man.

His fortunate escape raised the spirits of Asher, who still veering toward land, used his paddle with astonishing strength and skill.

" Doubtless they are among the best of their tribe, but I can beat them, as any white man can beat any Indian at his own game——"

If proof were needed of the truth of the Canadian's warning, it came the next minute, when Asher, who was looking to the rear for his enemies, discovered another party of them in front. The familiar dip of paddles brought his head around like a flash, and there, looming out of the fog, was a second boat, so like the one from which he was fleeing, that he would have believed it the same had he not known that the thing was impossible,

The meeting was so sudden that he knew he had been seen, and the only escape lay in the means he had just used. Without a second's hesitation, he headed his canoe toward the shore, and bent all the strength and cunning of his nature to the task.

"I must take to the woods," was his thought, "though, if they begin firing, I may not get the chance, but here goes!"

It was a mistake to suppose that the boat from which he had just fled contained the best canoeists, for the second moved more swiftly. Still, although Asher drew away from it more slowly, he none the less outsped it, and, could the race have continued as it began, it would not have taken him long to leave it out of sight.

His dread was that some of them would fire at him. The drizzling fog made it hard for the hunter of the olden time to keep his powder dry, but by care he could do so. The distance between the two boats was so short that a shot was almost sure to be fatal.

The young man could not know how far he had to go before reaching shore, but his hope was that he would not do so until beyond sight of his enemies, for it was important that they should not know the precise point where he landed, since they might be upon him before he could get away or hide himself.

It was with something like dismay, therefore, that while his last pursuers were still dimly in sight, he caught the outlines of land, with the dripping branches impending over the water.   Looking back a moment later, he saw that the large canoe was still visible.

Still worse, the first boat came into sight again. The cunning occupants had been quick to catch the situation, and the two were now converging upon him.   At best, he could not make land more than a few seconds in advance.

And worst of all, just as he had headed his little craft for the overhanging limb, a third boat put out from the exact spot!   He was surrounded, and escape was impossible.

" It 's all up! " was his exclamation, as he ceased paddling and resigned himself to his fate.

CHAPTER XVI.

WALLED IN.

AFTER all it was only what might have been expected. Asher Norris had set out to do an impossible thing. Not only did he fail to bring any relief to the missing Madge Linwood, but he himself was taken captive. Her parents had given, even amidst their grief, the soundest of advice.

It was an extraordinary conjunction of circumstances that brought this calamity upon him. He had proved his ability to outspeed the first canoe that discovered him, and was drawing away more slowly from the second. Slight as was his start, there was still a chance that, after leaping ashore, among the dense undergrowth and trees, where the darkness was impenetrable, he could save himself; but the sudden appearance of a third boat issuing from the very spot toward which he was aiming, and which he had almost reached, dashed every hope to the earth.

There was a single instant when he gathered his energies for a desperate dive into the water, with a view of coming up where he would not be observed, but his enemies were too close on every hand. He laid down his paddle beside his rifle in the bottom of the canoe, folded his arms and resigned himself to the inevitable.

The three large canoes so graduated their speed that in a few seconds they were on the sides and in front. There were muttered expressions of pleasure over the capture, and it was with feelings which may perhaps be imagined that the young man recognized the voice of Gray Wolf, who came so near making a captive of him the night before. He was in the boat that had last come to view, darting out from the overhanging vegetation along the shore. Apparently he was the most delighted of the entire party, for he uttered several exclamations in his own tongue and moved about with a childish exuberance of spirits rarely seen in any of his race.

It is at critical moments that the mind is most susceptible to trifles. Sitting with arms folded and half expecting one or more of the hostiles to sink their tomahawks in his brain, the prisoner counted, twice over, the three parties that converged around him. There were eight in the first canoe, seven in the second, and five in the last. Could the bravest man be censured for surrendering to a score of his armed enemies ?

It might look like a compliment to the young

man that none of his captors offered him violence, but he was too wise to take that view. To have slain him then and there would have been the end of it all. The American Indian does not favor that method of disposing of prisoners. There are sweet possibilities in the way of torture which tempt them to make the most of their opportunities. Besides, Pontiac himself would expect to be consulted as to the disposal of this sturdy young man.

One of the warriors placed his hand on the gunwale of Asher's canoe, and the three paddled slowly down stream, not halting until an open space was reached, which served as a sort of dock for the Canadian residents. Here the prows touched land, and, obeying a gruff command in broken English, the prisoner stepped ashore, followed by a half dozen of the hostiles. He was allowed to retain his rifle, and as yet no one laid hand upon him.

A conference among the party lasted for some minutes, the purpose no doubt being to decide upon the right course to follow. At the conclusion, most of the Indians re-entered their canoes and paddled swiftly out upon the river, where they passed from sight. The signs were that the Canadian told the truth about Pontiac having important business on hand that night.

Five warriors were left in charge of Asher Norris, and, without delay, they set out for the Ottawa encampment, which it will be remembered was in the rear of the Canadian settlement. To reach it they passed between the houses and into the wood beyond. The slight attention which they attracted from the settlers showed how accustomed they were to see the Indians that were besieging Fort Detroit. One or two greetings were exchanged between acquaintances, but the redmen moved forward without turning to the right or left, except as some obstruction presented itself, until they reached their village.

This aboriginal settlement consisted of more than a hundred lodges, made of bark and skins, in which lived the Ottawa warriors and their families. Accustomed as they were to the migratory life which is one of the characteristics of the American Indian, these people were ready to move at any hour of the day or night. It is known that Pontiac made more than one such removal of tribes after laying siege to Detroit.

It has been shown that he obtained many of his supplies from the Canadian neighbors, while a number of warriors could be spared most of the time to fish in the river, where they were always successful, or to hunt in the woods with its abundance of game. So the besiegers of the frontier post were never in danger of suffering, because of lack of food, as was the case more than once with those whom they besieged.

There is little of an attractive nature to be found

in an Indian encampment. The people have never been noted for their cleanliness, and their manner of living is only a little above that of the animals of the woods. The conical tents made of skins, sometimes banked around with dirt in winter, are supported by several poles, spread apart at the bottom and joined at the top, where an opening allows the smoke to go out and the rain and snow to come in. Peltries, and sometimes the bare ground, serve as couches, the choicest being appropriated by the head of the primitive household, who smokes and grunts and eats and sleeps, while his squaw does the work and drudgery.

There was a slight modification of the usual method of living, because the Ottawas, like the other tribes in the neighborhood, were on the war-path. They were not at home as often as usual, for their chief had something for them to do, and they were doing it with appropriate energy. Thus it happened that often at night there were not twenty warriors in the village, while again there might be ten times that number.

It was another evidence of the truth of the Canadian's words that when Asher Norris entered the Ottawa encampment few other persons were present except the women and children. Important movements evidently were on foot, and the men were needed elsewhere.

It did seem to Asher that his captors were able to read his thoughts. He knew when the start was made from the shore that they meant to take him to their village, and he resolved that if the slightest chance offered he would make a dash for freedom. But the chance did not offer. The Indians so disposed themselves that they were on every side, and at the first movement on his part he would have been not only checked but savagely stricken to the ground. So he walked as peaceably to the encampment as if he lived there and was returning to his own home.

The action of his captors indicated that they had already selected his prison, for with the same directness as before, they picked their way amid the tepees, from a number of which glowed the dull light of fires, to a lodge near the centre of the village. The leading warrior, who was Gray Wolf, drew aside the flap and said:

" Go in, lay down, rest! "

Asher ducked his head to obey. As he was passing the Indian reached out and laid his hand on his gun. The youth was hopeful that he would still be allowed to retain it, but such indulgence would have been remarkable. He could not resist, and so his cherished weapon went into the possession of his bitter enemy. He was allowed to keep his hunting knife, but its value was not to be compared with that of the other weapon.

One surprise followed another. Naturally he expected to find persons in the tepee, but he was entirely alone. The tent was five or six yards in diameter, made of buffalo skins, with the furry side turned inward. Through the opening in the apex of the cone the chilling rain trickled to the earth, just missing the fire that was burning a little to one side of the middle of the apartment. This fire had been recently replenished, for its warmth and glow filled the interior.

The other evidence of occupancy was a couple of buffalo robes at one side of the lodge, upon which, after a brief hesitation, Asher seated himself with a sigh, half of wonderment and half of despair.

" Well," he said grimly, " I set out for the Ottawa village, and I have reached it; I certainly have been successful so far, but what lies beyond ? "

Aye, that was the question.

He surveyed the interior of the lodge more critically. Although the fire was burning strongly, there was a pile of wood near at hand, so that more could be used when needed. On the other side of the fire lay a tomahawk that had evidently been used in breaking the fuel, but there was no sign of recent cooking, and, but for the blankets on which he was seated, he would have believed that the tepee had just been put up and was awaiting occupancy.

After his entrance, Gray Wolf had let the flap of

the tent fall back, so that it may be said the prisoner was walled in, the only door thus being closed. True, his hunting knife would open a new egress at any part of the wall, but it was not likely to prove of advantage to him, since it was unsupposable that his captors would leave him wholly to himself.

Here and there the sides of the tepee had been patched, the thread employed being deer sinews, so that it was quite compact and secure, with the exception of the chimney, through which the misty rain continued to find its way. On the whole, his treatment up to this point was far more considerate than he had a right to expect.

The belief of Asher Norris was that he would be left alone until morning, or at least until Pontiac's wishes could be known. The chief was absent with his warriors and was not likely to return for a number of hours. When he should do that, the young man would speedily learn his fate.

This decision on his part gave him abundance of time to reflect upon the errand that had been the cause of his mishap. His heart gave a quicker throb at the thought that Madge was probably at that moment within sound of his voice.

" It may be she is in the adjoining lodge," he added, turning his head, as if he half expected to see her.

" Yes, she may be," he added the next minute,

" but she might as well be a mile distant, for all the good I can do her."

He reclined upon the furs, and, leaning his head on his elbow, gazed into the fire, bitterly reflecting upon the cruel fate that had overtaken him. But it was only a characteristic of human nature that the uppermost thought in his mind was that of escape. Desperate as was the outlook, he could not believe the chance was wholly absent. He was too sensible to believe that his enemies were not watching around the tepee, alert for such attempt on his part. It might be indeed that they hoped to tempt him to make the essay.

But as the night progressed he intended to allow the fire to sink; most of the people in the village would be asleep; instead of passing out of the door, he would cut an opening through the skins at the rear of his couch and steal noiselessly out into the darkness, leaping to his feet and making off before the sentinels knew what he was doing.

This, apparently, was a reasonable scheme, but it must await the critical test. Occasionally he heard sounds of voices, and now and then the step of some Indian as he slouched past the tepee, but these disturbances became less frequent, and after a time it seemed as if slumber had settled upon the whole village.

The fire had smouldered until the dull illumination barely filled the dismal interior.   At first Asher flung a few sticks on the blaze, but after it had died out again he decided to let it alone.   The drizzling rain ceased and the wind soughed mournfully through the forest, while the stillness became so profound that it was easy to fancy himself in the depth of the solitude, with every living person hundreds of miles distant.

"I may be doing wrong," thought the young man, whose nerves were too wrought up for him to sleep, "but I'll try it."

CHAPTER XVII.

WHO WAS SHE?

AS near as Asher Norris could judge it was about midnight. The few embers at the side of the lodge cast flickering shadows through the interior and against the furs that composed the walls of the aboriginal structure. For an hour he had heard nothing of his enemies, the only sounds being the mournful sighing of the night wind through the branches of the trees. The Indian village, unlike many others, seemed to be altogether wanting in dogs, for not a howl or bark broke upon the hollow silence.

Once the prisoner fancied he heard the reports of several guns from the direction of the fort. When they sounded again, he knew it was not fancy.

" Pontiac is at work; I cannot guess what his new plot is, but surely he will not find Major Gladwyn unprepared; the months that have passed have given him time to learn every possible wile of the wretches."

The plan of the captive has already been intimated; it was to slit the buffalo wall at his side, so

as to allow him to pass through.   To rise to his feet
and walk or even leap to the door would be to leap
as it were into the arms of his foes.   That they
would be quick to learn of his flight, if made as he
contemplated, was self evident.   His chance, therefore, lay in his celerity of movement.   It was reasonable to believe that, vigilant as were the sentinels,
none of them was immediately at the spot where he
intended to make his dash for freedom.   Once upon
the outside, his reliance was upon the stygian darkness and his own skill in concealing his movements.

Before acting, he revolved another scheme in
mind.   That was to roll up one of the buffalo robes
so that in the obscurity, it would be mistaken for
his body, by those that were peering into the tent.
The difficulty, however, in this was that the action
necessary was almost sure to draw attention and
rouse suspicion.

" It won't do," was his conclusion.

He was lying on his side, with his face turned so
that he could see the fire and the flap beyond.
Occasionally the latter trembled, as if from the
wind, though it was so faintly seen in the obscurity
that the cause might have been something else,
without his being able to determine the fact.

Twice Asher Norris fancied he heard a slight
noise, whose nature he could not understand.   It
was so faint that he could not fix the point whence

it came, though of necessity it was outside the tepee. He turned his head in different directions, and was annoyed at his failure to identify it. Finally he concluded that it was made by something rubbing against the outside of the lodge.

With this belief came little enlightenment, though it raised a new hope. At first he thought it might be a prowling animal, but the disturbance was not such as would have been produced by that cause. The result of his intense listening was that at the end of a few more minutes he located the spot. It was between him and the smouldering fire; that is, not more than six feet beyond where his head was resting on the buffalo robe.

Some one was cutting into the side of the lodge!

Like a flash the truth came upon him, and almost stopped the beating of his heart, for with the knowledge was the belief that it was a friend that was trying in that cautious way to open communication, with a view of helping him to regain his freedom.

Acting on the impulse, Asher raised his head and peered intently toward the point. He regretted the sluggishness of the fire, for the light was so dim that he could discern nothing unusual, and, fearing he had done an imprudent thing, he sank back again, making his action like that of a person moving unconsciously in his sleep. He felt that he ought to have awaited further developments before letting it be known that he was aware of what was going on. Second thought convinced him that it was as likely to be a friend as an enemy at work.

That he was right in his supposition that some person was busy on the outside of the tepee was curiously demonstrated within the following two or three minutes. Although a chilly August storm had been raging for hours, the long-continued fire in the lodge made the interior close and warm. The small opening at the apex did not give sufficient draft to lower the atmosphere within.

There was a perceptible coolness in the air about his head. A slight current was coming in from the outside, and, passing over him, found its escape through the orifice at the top of the lodge. The inference was clear; an opening had been cut into the side of the tepee.

The slight abrading sound that had puzzled him was heard no more, for the reason that whoever was at work had finished. The opening was made.

This new intrusion upon his plans held the youth undecided what to do. He could not know whether a friend or an enemy was near him, and until some sign was made prudence suggested that he do nothing. The difficulty of seeing plainly in the dim light was increased by the fact that, as will be remembered, the fur sides of the buffalo robes composing the walls of the tepee were turned inward. These being of a dark color, so harmonized with the blackness of the outside that an opening a foot in diameter would not have been visible a couple of paces away. It was the inward flow of air that told the story.

There was an obvious remedy for this : he had but to reach out and throw some additional sticks on the fire. The flare would fill the interior with light and settle at once one part of the question. It was the fear that the individual was an enemy, who, mistaking the meaning of the action, would fire upon him. In truth, Asher had a shuddering dread that some foe, more malignant than the others, was seeking to slay him through this secret means.

This doubt, perplexity, and misgiving became such a strain upon his nerves that he would have been forced to end it by some means, had it not been terminated in a way as sudden as unexpected.

One of the smouldering embers fell apart, sending a glare through the tepee which lasted only a few seconds, but long enough to show not only the opening in the side, but a small, round, glistening object beyond which he knew was a human eye. Some one was peering through the slit at him. Not only that, but the person held the slight opening apart with his finger, the point of which was visible at the lower edge.

Whether he was a friend or enemy, Asher meant that he should know he was seen. Before the illumination had gone out, he raised himself on his elbow and looked straight at the eye which was looking at him. Then, as obscurity came again, he sank back on his couch, wondering what it all meant.

Once more an unexpected intervention had stopped the carrying out of the plan he had formed, and which he was on the eve of putting into execution. The presence of a man on the outside, so near to where the captive would have had to make his exit, showed the impossibility of escaping. Indeed, it was folly to suppose that after the party of Ottawas had made him captive and placed him in prison, they would allow him the slightest chance of getting away. To slash the robe and creep out, expecting to rise to his feet and make off, was as far beyond his power as it was to beat off the twenty warriors when they surrounded him in their canoes.

The shivering dread that one of the miscreants, probably Gray Wolf, was seeking the means of secretly slaying him, led Asher to roll aside and to jumble up the robes, which he hoped would be mistaken for his body in the gloom and receive the shot intended for him. But no such shot was fired, and he listened, thinking that the Indian might make another opening closer to him through which to thrust his arm and strike him with his knife.

" He shall not find me unprepared for that,"
muttered the youth with compressed lips, half wishing the attempt might be made.

There was but one conclusion to reach; escape
was out of the question, at least on this night and
under these circumstances, and he could only wait
and trust to heaven, to which he appealed, that the
future might open some way out of his affliction.

" Good heavens! why did I not think of it ? "

The light broke upon him like a lightning's flash.
The finger which he had looked upon for a moment, as
it curled over the lower part of the slit in the buffalo
robe, was small and well shaped.   He saw enough of
it to notice that.   It could not have been the finger
of a warrior or of a man, but belonged to a woman.

Who was she ?

Strange that the fact did not impress him at the
time.   How blind he was not to see that which
should have been as notable as the glistening of the
eye itself!

Could it have been Madge Linwood ?

The question almost took away his breath.   For one
moment he was certain it was she, but sober reflection
is a great dampener of hope, and he was speedily
forced to see that such could not have been the fact.

" If Madge is in this village, she would not be
permitted the liberty that would allow her to do a
thing like that.   Above all, had it been she, she

would have spoken or found some way of letting me know it!"

A second female came into his thoughts—Catharine, the Ojibwa girl, the supposed friend of Pontiac and the Ottawas, but the invaluable friend of the imperilled white men at Detroit. She was permitted full freedom of action, and there was nothing improbable in the thought that she had taken this method of gaining sight of the hapless prisoner. Not wishing the sentinels to know that she had any interest in or cared for him, she refrained from entering by way of the door, but cut a hole in the skin wall in order to identify the captive. Fortunately the raising of his head at the moment of the temporary lighting up of the room made that identification positive.

" Catharine learned that the Ottawas had brought in a prisoner, and, waiting until she was believed to be asleep, she set out to learn who he was. Can it be that Madge heard the news, and sent her ?"

It was a perplexing situation in which the youth found himself, and while still striving to find his way out of the labyrinth, he fell asleep. Nature will assert herself, and he did not open his eyes again until the sun was above the horizon.

It took several minutes for Asher to recall the events of the preceding night, and to remember where he was. When he looked about him, he saw that he had company. A squaw, bent, haggard, and gaunt, fully three-score and ten years of age, had started the fire afresh and was cooking some kind of meat over the blaze, by skewering it upon sticks and holding it above the flames. Asher rose to a sitting posture and called out:

" Good morning! "

The old woman acted as if she did not hear him, and thought him still asleep.

" White people are not the only ones who become deaf," thought the youth ; " I wish I had some water for my hands and face, but what 's the use of asking a person who cannot hear a word ? At any rate, I 'm hungry, and that meat smells good."

He held his sitting position until she looked round and saw him. As he met her eye, he nodded, but the little twinkling bead-like orbs seemed to be blind, for she gave no response. The meat was prepared, and she suddenly flung it toward him.

Asher caught it on the fly, and speedily ate it with the relish that youth and high health gave.

" Thank you; it is very good, mother."

She had employed herself in eating, and did not finish as soon as the prisoner, who was still watching her with curious interest, when the flap of the door was drawn aside and an Indian warrior strode into the tepee.

One glance at the intruder was sufficient: he was Pontiac, chief of the Ottawas.

CHAPTER XVIII.

PONTIAC.

PONTIAC, chief of the Ottawas, was of medium height, rather stockily built, with strong features, which would have been less attractive but for their stamp of intellectuality and their unmistakable impress of greatness. No one could look at that face without noting his superiority over his followers. There was a flash of the black eye, a curl of the thin lips, a knitting of the brows and a general air of thoughtfulness and a lofty bearing which marked him as a born leader.

But this famous sachem lacked the fine ingrained nobility which distinguished Tecumseh, the Shawanoe. While he had many of the traits that his partisans lacked, he possessed all their vices, the cunning, and the treachery which are characteristics of his race. His burning ambition was to destroy or at least to injure the white people, and in carrying out that resolution, no consideration of honor nor any plighted word interposed. When messengers went to him from Major Gladwyn at his own request to confer over their trouble, he held them prisoners and put one to death. The other would have been slain had he not effected his escape. Pontiac professed the warmest friendship for the commandant, while plotting the massacre of himself and garrison. His first visit, under the guise of good will, was intended, as we have shown, to open the way for slaying every white person in Detroit. He was brave but treacherous, able but dishonorable, and shrewd, but altogether untrustworthy.

Few understood the chieftain better than Asher Norris, who, recognizing the head and front of the gigantic conspiracy, as he entered the lodge, promptly rose to his feet and made a military salute. They had met before and knew each other well. Aware that the Ottawa spoke English fluently, the youth addressed him:

" I greet my brother, the great leader of the Ottawas and of other tribes who are proud to fight under Pontiac."

As an impromptu this was creditable in the way of compliment, of which the American Indian is fond, but it may have been that it was because Pontiac was so accustomed to flattery that it produced no visible effect. He looked steadily into the face of the youth who met the gaze unflinchingly while waiting for him to respond.

" Why is the white man in the lodge of Wamo-aka ? " was the demand, as if Asher had forced his presence into a place where it was not welcome.

"The warriors of Pontiac took me a prisoner last night and brought me here; if it is the will of Pontiac that I shall depart, I will do so."

But it was hardly to be supposed that the chieftain held any such wish.   He was not in the habit of returning prisoners.

"Where was the white man when my warriors made him captive?" he asked.

"In my canoe, paddling on the river."

"Why in your canoe and paddling on the river?"

"One of the fathers at Detroit has lost his daughter; the hearts of the parents are sad because she comes not back to them; I was looking for her."

"Did the white man find her?"

"I did not; I have not seen her; I know not where she is."

Asher doubted whether these words were wise. If Pontiac learned that he loved Madge Linwood, his hatred would be inflamed.   Probably he had brought about the death of Pierre Muire because the Canadian had dared to love her, but, on the other hand, it was not to be doubted that the chief intended to slay his prisoner without this additional incentive.   Consequently Asher was in the deplorable dilemma which could be made no worse by any word or act of his.

He hoped to gain a clue in the reply of the sachem, but was disappointed.

" The white man has not the eye of the Indian: he cannot see in the night, like the owl and the Ottawa."

" The words of Pontiac are true; I have not seen the child of my friend; the eyes of Pontiac are keener than those of the white man."

Still the chief refused to accept the hint.

" Does the white man love the daughter of the pale faces ?"

It was a startling question, whose meaning Asher Norris penetrated, but he cleverly parried the danger.

" All who know the child of my friend love her, for she is good and kind; the redmen and women love her and would shield her from harm."

The glittering eyes of the chieftain flashed, and his thin lips closed over his teeth. He seemed to look through his prisoner. Almost any one would have quailed before that burning gaze, but the youth did not waver. He sought to give the impression that he suspected no wrong and trusted the chief, when in truth he looked upon him as he would have looked upon a coiled rattlesnake.

It would have been interesting could any one have interpreted the thoughts that surged in the brain of the dusky leader, but who but himself could do so ? Asher read the meaning of his question, but he had evaded an answer with no little skill.   If he supposed, however, the sachem would rest content with preliminary defeat, he was mistaken.

" Does the white man love her more than do others ? "

Having in mind the parents of Madge, Asher felt he was speaking only the truth, when he replied:

" No; she is good to all; therefore all love her."

Deceitful and untruthful himself, Pontiac (as was proved by his subsequent course) did not believe these words; but he must have seen that it was idle to pursue that line further.

" Major Gladwyn is an evil man," he said, abruptly changing the range of his remarks; " he speaks with a double tongue; he is like the serpent in the grass which strikes when no one sees it."

There was no way of agreeing with this sentiment without violating truth, which Asher Norris would not do to save his own life.   Major Gladwyn was not a man to speak with a " double tongue," for his sense of honor was exalted.   It was Pontiac that had gone to him with lies on his lips.

" All men speak with a double tongue, when the Great Spirit tells them to do so," was the rather lame declaration of the captive; " when the redman wishes to outwit the white man he makes a cloud before his eyes so that the white man does not see that which hides his face."

Possibly Pontiac saw in these words a veiled allusion to himself, but, if so, he did not resent it.

" Detroit will soon be gone! " he exclaimed with an energy as sudden as it was startling; " the fort and all the houses shall be burned and the white men and women shall become the prisoners of Pontiac."

The high spirit of the prisoner would not allow him to accept this bombast without protest. Why attempt to curry favor with a miscreant whom nothing could induce to be merciful or chivalrous ?

" Pontiac has spoken these words many times; why does he wait ? "

" Because he is merciful; he will give the white men and women time to prepare for that which they know is coming."

This was truly an aboriginal way of stating the case, but it was hardly convincing to the prisoner.

" Pontiac has tried to capture the fort, but he failed; Major Gladwyn is stronger than before. He has more men; he has powder; he has plenty of food."

" It is a lie! He has not more men! Where is Dalzell ? Where are the hundred white men who fell with him ? The white man speaks lies! "

In one sense Pontiac had truth on his side, for unquestionably Detroit was weaker than just before the fearful repulse at Bloody Ridge, but Asher Norris referred to the steady and certain improvement in the situation of the besieged fort.

" Pontiac speaks with a single tongue : many of the white men fell with Major Dalzell, as did many warriors, but others have come ; the palisades and the fort are strong; the sentinels do not sleep; they have more powder and bullets than they need; they have no fear of Pontiac and his warriors; they know they are safe."

Certainly these were brave words under the circumstances, and Asher was doubtful as to their reception, but the chieftain seemed inclined to wordy rather than physical warfare.

" The redmen are like the leaves on the trees; they are coming to Pontiac; the Pottawatomies, the Wyandots and Ojibwas are here; the Sioux are on the war-path; the chiefs of the Creeks and Choctaws and their warriors fill a thousand canoes that are hurrying up the Mississippi to Pontiac; the Iroquois, the children of Hiawatha, whose name makes the white men tremble, are treading the forests from the great water toward the rising sun, with their faces toward Detroit; when they come they will crush Major Gladwyn and his soldiers like the grasshoppers in their path."

Of this tremendous boast it may be said that it was " important, if true." That Pontiac would secure more allies was extremely probable, but in the meantime, what of the defenders of Detroit ?

Page 177.   AN UNEXPECTED FRIEND.

" The redmen are but a handful to the white men; King Philip tried to slay them, when they were few, but he was killed and his warriors driven into the wilderness; it will be so again with Pontiac; does he think that Major Gladwyn has been forgotten by his white brothers ? No; they will send thousands of soldiers with little and big guns, so that the redmen will flee in affright to the woods."

By this time the chieftain must have concluded that his prisoner was capable of drawing as long a bow as he. Instead of replying with another vaunt, he continued looking into his countenance with the same piercing gaze, while Asher Norris met the look with an unwavering stare. Meanwhile, the old woman, who was probably Wa-mo-aka, had left the tepee, and the two were alone.

The position of the captor and captive was such that the back of the former was toward the flap which served as a door, while the youth faced it. It was at this point in the conversation that Asher saw the flap pulled noiselessly aside for the space of a few inches, a face thrust forward and immediately withdrawn.

Brief as was the interval, it was sufficient for him to identify the countenance. It was Catharine, the Ojibwa maiden, and he no longer doubted that it was she who, after cutting the slip in the side of the tepee the night before, had looked through and recognized him by the glare of the expiring ember.

Pontiac had his knife and tomahawk at his waist, but the upper part of his body was bare and he did not carry his rifle. His chest, like his face, was daubed with streaks of red, yellow, and black paint, which added to the hideousness of his appearance. He allowed his arms to hang loosely at his sides while speaking, except that now and then, when excited, he used them for gesture.

Most of the time Asher Norris kept his arms folded, for in that way his right hand rested against the handle of his knife, which, as in the case of most of the frontiersmen, was suspended over his heart, though some of them carried it in the girdle at the waist like the Indians. The youth believed the chief would become ungovernably incensed by his words, and would rush upon him with upraised knife.

" If he does so," was his thought, " there will be a dead Pontiac before Asher Norris takes his departure from this life. I shall not stand idle, or meekly try to escape, but will fight him with might and main."

It is hardly to be supposed that the Ottawa had any suspicion of the resolution of the captive, despite his undaunted demeanor, or that, if he did suspect it, he would have been frightened from an assault, for, as has been stated, no one who knew Pontiac ever questioned his personal bravery. He was restrained by other causes that were soon to become known.

Instead of replying to the last boast of Asher, Pontiac, after surveying him for a few seconds, turned and walked to the entrance. The hanging door was drawn aside, and he stooped and passed out. Then halting and holding the flap away, he beckoned with his other hand for Asher to follow him.

Without a moment's hesitation, the prisoner obeyed.

CHAPTER XIX.

IT will be recalled that at no point in this remarkable conversation did Asher Norris show any fear of the terrible Pontiac who held him at his mercy. It was with the same dauntless demeanor he had shown from the first that he obeyed the gesture of the chief to follow him from the tepee of Wa-mo-aka. Striding across the brief space he lowered his head, passed through the entrance and paused on the outside, where the leader of the Ottawas awaited him.

There is nothing that the American Indian likes more than unflinching bravery. Had the youth whined and begged for mercy it is quite probable that he would have been smitten to the earth, but when he stood up before the chieftain, as if courting a personal combat, Pontiac lost his malignant hatred for the moment in admiration of the splendid courage of the youth.

But, while all this was true, it must not be supposed that the savage held any purpose of rewarding his prisoner for his unusual demeanor by

180

presenting him with his freedom. Such is not the nature of the redman.

The sun was shining, and the scene around the two was of strange interest and activity. The tepees had been set up in the woods, whose exuberant vegetation allowed but few rays of sunlight to pierce their branches. The numerous tents, of which Wa-mo-aka's may be taken as a type, were placed as the location of the tree trunks compelled, so that there was no semblance of symmetry or regularity. Squaws were passing to and fro, children playing and running among the trees, warriors lounging here and there, most of them smoking, but a large number were engaged in cleaning their guns as if preparing for some warlike expedition. Amid all the bustle and activity there were no signs, as far as Asher could note, of the important enterprise of the evening before. If there had been fighting, the Ottawas must have suffered in killed and wounded. But he had heard no sounds of wailing or mourning on the previous night, nor was anything of the kind now present. It looked as if the enterprise, whatever its nature, had been abandoned.

The personality of Pontiac was always interesting to his followers, but the awe in which he was held prevented any obtrusive curiosity as to the prisoner with whom he started on a walk in the direction of the river. Every eye seemed to be turned upon the two as they picked their way in and out among the tepees, but there was more of shrinking back than of pressing forward. No one ventured to address the chief, who did not speak until clear of the village.

It was then but a short distance to the Canadian settlement, which intervened between the Indian encampment and the Detroit river; but instead of going through that fringe of cabins, Pontiac turned to the right, as if he meant to pass round the upper end, and thus avoid meeting any who were of the same race as his prisoner.

Asher had plenty of cause for speculation during this singular journey, for the chief did not speak nor give any intimation as to its meaning, but the youth was alert, and it was a striking proof of his acuteness that he made an important discovery, unsuspected by his captor.

With his thoughts dwelling often upon Madge Linwood, Asher glanced sharply on every hand while picking his way among the tepees in the hope of gaining sight of her. Though he failed, he discovered something else of great significance.

Several Indians were following him and Pontiac. There were two on the right hand and the same number on the left, all deftly dodging among the trees so as nearly to keep pace with the two, and doing it so skilfully that few beside Asher Norris would have noticed them. The uncomforting conviction came to the prisoner that he was being led to his execution, a conviction that was strengthened when he recognized one of the four as his enemy, Gray Wolf.

Without trying to determine the best thing to do, if indeed he could do anything, Asher decided to be governed by circumstances. If he was doomed to die there was no help for it, but whatever his fate, he would go down with colors flying.

At the point where they had to turn in order to follow the most direct route to the river, the two emerged into a small natural clearing of a few hundred feet in extent. There Pontiac abruptly halted, and, turning upon his companion, said :

" The white man has a knife; Pontiac has a knife; they shall learn who is the bravest, and who shall fall to the earth."

This sounded very much like a challenge to mortal combat. Asher Norris would not have hesitated for an instant to accept the gage of battle, could he have received chivalrous treatment, but he now saw the meaning of the four warriors stealthily following them to this point. They were to watch the combat, and the moment it should become necessary to interfere for their chief, they would do so. The whole thing was a characteristic piece of Indian trickery.

" I will fight Pontiac, and will not ask mercy of

him, but is Pontiac the brave man he is said to be, when he brings four of his warriors to help him fight one white man ? ''

It is rarely that an Indian manifests surprise, but the chieftain did so in this instance, immediately rallying and asking as he looked about him:

'' Where are the warriors that the white man tells about ? ''

'' They followed us from the village of the Ottawas; they did so by Pontiac's orders; they are hiding among the trees.''

Before the chief could make answer to this pointed declaration, two Indians emerged from the woods on the farther side of the clearing, and approached. A glance showed that they were not Ottawas, but belonged to some tribe which Asher did not identify. They had just reached the neighborhood with a large band of warriors, and had set out to find Pontiac for consultation.

'' Huh ! '' exclaimed the pleased sachem as he recognized them. Their coming was unexpected, and all the more gratifying on that account. He stared for a moment and then took several paces forward to meet them, forgetting in his excitement the security of his prisoner.

'' Let Pontiac speak with his brothers,'' Asher was quick to say; '' I will await his pleasure.''

The pledge was kept. It seemed to be a chival-

rous one, but no credit should be given to the youth
who made it. He would have been off like a flash,
at the first opportunity, but for the presence of
those four sneaking wretches, only a few rods away
among the trees, who would have welcomed the
excuse for bringing him wounded to the earth and
then torturing him afterwards.

The coming of the strange chiefs was a surprise
to every one else, and of necessity postponed the
scheme that Pontiac had in mind regarding his prisoner. At best, it was a curious act on his part to
take a white man beyond his village for the sake of
engaging in a personal combat with him, when there
were many more convenient ways of disposing of
him.

It could not have been any faith in the pledge of
his captive that led Pontiac to walk away from him,
thus leaving him seemingly alone, but he knew that
his faithful lieutenants would keep keen watch over
him for any length of time.

Asher was so assured that he would not be harmed
while the interview lasted that he studied Pontiac
and his two visitors with keen interest. As the
three chiefs came together they greeted one another
with words uttered in low tones, while Pontiac
partly inclined his head, as if he had caught the
trick from the white people, but there was no shaking of hands or any other form of salutation. The

painted faces were aglow with pleasing excitement, for the new arrivals were as ardent in the cause of the Ottawa as he himself.

One of the chiefs was the finest Indian that Asher had ever seen. He was tall, graceful, with unusually regular features, and, curious as it may sound, the paint which he had spread on his breast and face displayed some taste, so that it could hardly be said that it disfigured his countenance, an accomplishment rarely, if ever, known when the aborigines of this country attempt to wield the artist's brush.

The three talked with much earnestness and gesture. It was in truth a council of war in which doubtless the commanding general explained to his lieutenants his plan of grand campaign. They must have felt unlimited faith in his prowess and pledges, to bring their warriors so great a distance to take part in the siege of Detroit, and, if looks could tell anything, that confidence and enthusiasm were intensified during the spirited interview.

Suddenly Pontiac seemed to decide to go with his visitors to view the reinforcements they had brought to him. He took several steps to do so, when he recalled the prisoner whom he had brought to the spot. He must have expected to find him gone, judging from his half-scared look as he wheeled about; but there stood the young man with folded arms, coolly contemplating him and his companions

as if awaiting an invitation to join in their consultation.

Pontiac did not intend to take his captive with
him, nor was it worth his while to accompany him
back to the village. His remedy was at hand. At
a signal Gray Wolf and his three companions
emerged from the wood into the clearing and drew
near. As they approached, Asher Norris cast a
meaning look at the Ottawa chieftain, for the incident was confirmatory of his charge, but the reproof
was thrown away since Pontiac saw nothing of which
to be ashamed in the proceeding.

There was a few minutes' talk between the leader
and Gray Wolf, who nodded his head to signify that
his wishes were understood. Then Pontiac strode
off with his visitors, quickly passing from sight
among the trees.

Once more Gray Wolf was the custodian of Asher,
who in obedience to a gesture turned his face toward
the Ottawa village and began retracing his steps.
He had noted one trifling thing which caused him
more annoyance than would be supposed: the rifle
that Gray Wolf carried was the handsome weapon
belonging to the prisoner.

On the return journey Gray Wolf walked immediately in front of the captive, the other three
being at the rear. Thus Asher had the humiliation
of seeing his rifle continually before his eyes, while

the detested figure of the thief was as continually
present in his vision.   The warriors did not tempt
the white man to make a dash for freedom, for that
would have necessitated violence on their part, for
which Pontiac would call them to account.   The
Ottawa leader was the strictest of autocrats among
his people.

Now that he was not with the prisoner, the rabble
of the village, as they may be called, gave unre-
strained attention to him.   The scowling warriors
watched him as he passed, and the women and
children drew near with many remarks, evidently
not of a complimentary nature, while some of their
actions were threatening.

Suddenly Asher received a resounding blow over
his shoulder.   He turned angrily, and saw a grinning
squaw with a stick in hand, as if asking him how he
liked it.   He could offer no resistance, but continued walking toward Wa-mo-aka's lodge, with as
much dignity as befitted the occasion.   Bang! came
a second blow, and this time it was struck by another squaw, who did not mean to be surpassed at
that kind of amusement.   Then several large and
small boys joined in, so that in a twinkling, as may
be said, Asher was running the gauntlet.   He would
have been vastly relieved had he dared to wheel
about and knock his tormentors right and left, but
that would have been unwise, and he bore his perse-

cution as philosophically as he could, scorning to break into a run.

Gray Wolf and his companions made no objection to the outrage, but fortunately the tepee was not far off, and a few minutes later Asher hurried through the entrance, no one daring to follow him.

" What 's to be the end of this ? " he muttered, flinging himself down on the buffalo robes; " there must be an end very soon——"

He caught his breath, for at that moment the flap was lifted again, and Madge Linwood stood before him.

CHAPTER XX.

MADGE.

A SHER NORRIS would have rushed forward
to clasp Madge Linwood in his arms, but she
spoke before he recovered from his shock of amazement:

"Stay where you are, Asher," she said in a low
but earnest voice; "you must not seem too glad to
see me; our enemies are all around us."

He had risen to his feet and paused with several
paces between them. The old squaw was absent,
but was liable to return at any moment, and even
while the girl spoke she saw several eyes at the
opening made in the side of the lodge by the knife
of Catharine, the Ojibwa maiden, as if there was
a strife among the spectators as to which should
secure the best view.

"Madge!" exclaimed the youth in an awed
undertone; "how is it you dare come to me?"

"My lodge is only a short distance away; were
you hurt?"

"You mean just now? No, the bruises were
only sufficient to make me angry; is this the first
time you saw me?"

" No; I saw you when you walked past with Pontiac, but I dared not speak."

" I looked for you, Madge, not knowing whether or not I ought to be glad to see you in this accursed place. When were you brought here ? "

" To-day is Friday; it was on Monday night."

" What a woful mistake that you were allowed to come with Pierre! "

" But his mother was very ill; I fear she has died."

" Yes; she died the next morning."

" Alas; and yet it is well, for she did not know of the cruel taking off of her son."

" Then you knew he was killed ? "

" He was shot at my side; he started to take me home, as he promised, and was paddling hard when a canoe approached. There were three Indians in it. They said something to Pierre which I did not understand, but he was frightened. He began paddling as fast as he could, and they followed him. Their position was such that he was forced to head toward this side of the river. Pierre was a fine canoeist, and he drew away from them, though they paddled with might and main. When we ran under the bushes, Pierre said we were safe, and Gray Wolf could not harm us."

" Then that imp was in the business!" exclaimed Asher.

" Alas that he was! For Pierre had hardly said

the words when the Indian canoe darted into sight.
Gray Wolf raised his gun, and the next minute
Pierre was dead.   They lifted me out of the boat
and brought me here."

"It was a sad business," said Asher.   "The
canoe must have caught in the bushes, for I found
it drifting the next night."

The tears of genuine grief filled the eyes of the
youth, for he felt as not before the cruel injustice he
had done the Canadian of whom he had been so
jealous.   He was striving to return Madge to her
parents, and died in the performance of duty.   He
doubtless loved the girl, but had not forced his affection upon her.

She and Asher were standing with half the width
of the lodge between them.   He asked her to sit
down, but she shook her head, saying it was more
prudent to keep their feet.   There was no saying
how many eyes were watching them, and everything
would be reported to Pontiac.

"In whose lodge are you staying, Madge?"

"With the wife of Pontiac; he is away most of
the time, but she treats me with more kindness than
I had a right to expect."

These words sent a pang through the heart of
Asher, for he saw a meaning in them that she did
not suspect.

"You know why I am here?" he said, and, as she

inclined her head, he hurriedly told her what had befallen him from the time he learned she was missing.

" I have little fear for myself," she added, " for I do not think they intend me any more harm than to hold me captive for awhile, but, O Asher, my heart is crushed for you."

" We are both in danger, and yours is as great as mine."

" I cannot think so, for they have offered me no injury, while my heart stood still when I saw you go by with Pontiac, for I did not believe I would ever see you again."

" When did you learn I was your companion in captivity ? "

" Catharine, the Ojibwa maiden, told me that a white man was brought in last night, but she had not seen him and did not know who he was. My heart misgave me, and I begged her to find out who the captive was. She waited until late, and then stole up to the side of the lodge, when none of the sentinels on guard saw her, cut a hole and peeped through."

" There is the spot," said Asher, indicating the opening; " I saw her eye and the end of her finger as she looked in, but did not suspect who she was until a good while after. Madge, have you had any chance to get away ? "

13

She looked surprised and then grieved.

" Do you think if such came to me I would not seize it on the instant ?   I have lain awake the night through, praying for such a chance; I have been on the alert through the day, but not once did it appear; I am still waiting, but beginning to think that I shall have to stay with the Ottawas for a long time—that is, until they begin to think I am satisfied.   Then when their suspicion is less, the opportunity will come to me.   Ah, father and mother! How your hearts must ache for your Madge!"

And, giving way to her emotions, she buried her face in her hands, while the tears trickled between the fingers.

It was plain to Asher Norris that the girl had no thought of her real danger.   Pontiac was infatuated with Madge, and she, in her youth and innocence, did not dream of the possibility of such a thing. It was his duty to warn her.

" Madge, Catharine is your friend, as everybody is; she will do all she can to help you, and you must try equally hard to help her in trying to help you."

" I know what you say is true, but none of her people have ever suspected Catharine of being friendly to our race, and she must not run too much danger."

In those words glowed the sweet nature of Madge Linwood.   Her first thought was not of herself, but

of others. Undoubtedly the Ojibwa girl could do
a great deal for her, but Madge was ready to inter-
pose through fear that it might endanger the safety
of her dusky friend.

" Madge, Pontiac is in love with you, and means
to make you his wife! "

The fair cheek paled, the dark eyes grew wider;
she was silent a moment, and then gasped:

" In love with me! Means to make me his wife! "

" Yes; he will never permit you to return to your
parents; if you do not break away and make your
escape soon it will be too late."

" But, Asher, he has a wife! "

" What of that ? Have not many of the Indians
more than one wife ? Aye, some of them have
three and four squaws to serve them like beasts of
burden. He will suffer no man to interfere; that is
why he had poor Pierre Muire killed; he knew he
loved you."

" Pierre loved me! He never whispered such a
word."

" He was too noble to do so until he saw hope,
but I knew of his passion; so did Catharine. Has
she not spoken to you ?"

" Never of Pierre; she did drop a hint about
Pontiac; but I did not understand her meaning."

" You understand it now, Madge; God protect
you! "

" But he has said nothing of the kind to me—not so much as a single word."

" He can afford to wait, but he will not wait long; you will learn the whole fearful truth all too soon from his own accursed lips."

The revelation seemed too frightful for the girl fully to grasp at first, but, young as she was, her woman's intuition told her that the words just spoken were those of soberness and truth. Quicker than Asher expected she rallied from the shock.

" But if Pontiac feels thus towards me, he will continue to be kind."

" He will until you are compelled to say ' yes ' or ' no ' to him."

" And I will die a thousand times before saying ' yes.' Oh, the thought! "

And she shuddered as if from the touch of a loathsome serpent.

" But, Asher," she hastened to add, " I am safe for a while, even though it be brief, while you are in peril every hour."

" Think not of me, but of yourself; Catharine will help you and take the first opportunity to get away; more depends upon her than upon any one else."

" Why did not Pontiac return with you ? "

" Before we reached the river he met two chiefs belonging to other tribes; he went off to talk to them and Gray Wolf and the others brought me back."

The youth did not think it well to tell everything.

" But for that you would have been killed. He has only deferred your death. You must not stay here another night."

" Those are wise words, dear Madge, but am I not watched as closely as you ? Do you imagine that if but half a chance were offered I would not seize it ? "

" What has become of your Uncle Jo? "

" Jo Spain ? Ah, misfortunes come together. He left the fort without knowing that you were missing."

She made no reply, but looked thoughtfully at the ground between them. She was thinking deeply upon something, and he waited for her to explain. Having impressed her with a full sense of her own danger, he felt there was little more to say. She could now be depended upon to do all that was within the possibility of human endeavor.

" I wonder whether it is fortunate that new cares have come to Pontiac," she said as if communing with herself. " He will not disturb me perhaps for a day or two longer, but he may wish to rid himself of you. Asher, does Pontiac think—that—you— love me ? "

A strange thrill shot through the heart of the youth at these words, for it was the first time that anything of that nature had been said by either.   Mastering his emotion as best he could, he replied :

" He asked me the question."

" The wretch ! and what was your reply ? "

" I said ' yes,' but start not Madge; my answer was that every one who knew you loved you—his own people as well as those of our race; so how could I help feeling as did they ? I don't know whether that satisfied him, but he had to accept it. You can see how jealous he is of those who dare to look upon you with longing eyes."

" It must be as you say—it must be——"

A peculiar grunting sound struck upon their ears, as the flap of the tent was raised and Wa-mo-aka, the old squaw, entered. She looked keenly at the two, as if she did not understand the meaning of the scene, and then going over to the robes on which Asher Norris had been reclining, sat down.

" Can she understand us ? " he asked.

" She is totally deaf, and cannot speak a word of English."

" I have not yet asked how it was you were permitted to come from the tepee of Pontiac to visit me."

" I told you that he and his squaw are kind; they suffer me to go outside of their lodge when I choose, but I am closely watched ; she knows enough English to catch my meaning. So I told her I was going to speak to the prisoner of Pontiac, and she showed no wish to prevent me."

" How long may you stay ? "

" I have already stayed longer than I intended, but no harm can come from it, since Pontiac is not likely to return for a good while."

" And when he does return and learns where you have been ? "

" Is it not proper that one white captive should wish to speak to another, who is also unfortunate ? But I must go; good-by."

He had hardly time to respond to her parting words, when she was gone, and as she passed out of Wa-mo-aka's tent, the shadow of a great dread and the glow of a great hope rested on her sweet face.

CHAPTER XXI.

A PRAYER AND ITS ANSWER.

IT has been a characteristic of some of the greatest military leaders of history that they were as simple in their tastes as the privates under their command. The gaudy uniform, the pomp and show and parade belong, as a rule, to those whose deeds and achievements are in the future.

Pontiac, chief of the Ottawas, in his dress and manner of living was hardly to be distinguished from the thousand warriors who were ready to follow him to death " as to a festival." Had any inquirer entered the Indian village, which stood on the eastern bank of the Detroit river, more than one hundred years ago, in search of the remarkable sachem, he would have been obliged to make inquiry to locate the imperial wigwam. It was one among many, standing, as has been shown, but a short distance from the tepee of Wa-mo-aka, in which Asher Norris was held a prisoner.

Pontiac had but one wife—at least there was only one with him at the time he laid siege to the famous frontier post—and, like many other noted chieftains, he had no children. His squaw was in middle life, and of anything but prepossessing appearance. The life companion of the terrible man speedily learned of his savage and resistless nature. She would no more have dared to go contrary to his remorseless will than would any of the Ottawa warriors whom he led in battle.

When, therefore, Madge Linwood was brought to his lodge as a captive, the wife received her with apparent pleasure, for she knew it meant her own death to do otherwise. In her heart she may have hated with indescribable intensity the comely maiden of another race, upon whom she saw her husband looking with covetous eyes, but if so her lord and master saw nothing of it, while Madge herself was surprised and relieved to find apparent good-will where she looked for persecution.

So it was that the few days and nights which she spent in the lodge were as bearable as they could be to the homesick one, who longed for her own parents and friends, and to whom the captivity would have been a horrible nightmare, but for the hope, caused by the kindness from the couple, that she would soon be allowed to go to her own home.

Pontiac was a shrewd personage in more than one respect. He did not spend most of his time in the lodge, persecuting the captive with his attentions. To do that would have roused dislike, opposition, and hatred. He had seen her more than once in Detroit, when all was pleasant between the white and the redman, and even though she was so young he admired and in his own rough way loved her. He was aware that she knew he was the greatest among his race ; he believed he was the chosen Moses to lead the redmen to triumph, and that all the white people in Detroit would soon be at his mercy. When, then, he spared her parents and friends from the doom that awaited the rest, when he launched forth as a conquering and mighty leader, would she not be proud to stand by his side as his queen ?

All this, of course, is but speculation, but the acts of Pontiac lend reasonableness to the theory that such dreams guided his action for a few memorable days. When it is remembered that he was a barbarian, with the crude, wild imaginings of his people, addicted to the most extravagant day dreaming, with a brain surcharged with gorgeous and grotesque fancies, there is nothing incredible in the thought that he believed he could win the maiden of Caucasian blood without resort to the violence that he was ready to use as a last resort.

The intuition of the female mind is marvellous, and at times past comprehension, even in one so young as Madge Linwood or Catharine the Ojibwa, who was somewhat older than her civilized sister.

The revelation of Asher Norris, made at a critical moment, was neither too early nor too late. Even while talking with him her active brain evolved a line of action, creditable and even brilliant in conception.

In brief she saw, as she told him, that she was in no immediate danger, for she could dally with Pontiac for several days, but as for the youth, his life was not secure for an hour. It had been saved thus far by providential interference, but it was as idle to expect that to continue, as it was to look for a string of miracles, one after another and without end. Unless his release was brought about within the following twenty-four hours, or probably within less time, it would never come. Her thoughts, therefore, were concentrated upon the problem of securing that release.

There was but the one way possible; appeal to Pontiac himself, and beg of him as a favor that the young man should be sent back to his people. Would he not do so simple a thing in order to win her thanks and smiles ?

This, in brief, was the line she had determined to follow. When the idea first came into her mind, she was confident of its success. Suppose the chieftain set Asher free and permitted him to return to Detroit. In what possible way would the chief harm himself or imperil the scheme he had formed ?

He looked with contempt upon Major Gladwyn and his garrison, whose temporary safety lay in keeping as closely as possible behind the palisades.   He did not dare march out to attack any of the beleaguering tribes, so that no appeal of Asher Norris or of the friends of Madge Linwood could bring any danger of the fair captive being wrested from Pontiac.

This was the favorable view that first presented itself to her, but intense thought brought to light many " briers in the path."   She might truly claim that she would appeal for the same mercy at the hands of the chieftain, no matter who the hapless prisoner was, but the sagacious sachem was quite sure to read truly the deeper, tenderer feeling that actuated the girl, and a suspicion on his part that the youth dared to love the maiden would set aflame all the ungovernable ferocity of his nature against his more comely rival.   If he had ordered Pierre Muire to be shot, because of a hint that the Canadian presumed to be a rival even in thought, how much more merciless would he be toward the youth of whose sentiments there could be no doubt ?

So it was that poignant fear was mingled with hope.   She must, if possible, allay the suspicion of Pontiac, who, in his rage, might throw all dissemblance aside, slay Asher Norris and compel her to be his companion.   It was this dread which clouded her face, even while it glowed with hope, as she

bade Asher good-by and passed out of the lodge of
Wa-mo-aka to return to her own.

She longed for the companionship of Catharine
the Ojibwa. She could fully trust her and needed
her counsel. The two together could plan better
than apart and unaided. Catharine was in the
lodge when Madge left it a short time before, for
that historical character, whose friendship for the
whites seemed never to have been suspected by her
own people, wandered at will among the different
nationalities, as Pontiac himself might have done.

But Catharine was absent ; and when Madge
inquired of the wife of Pontiac, that woman in her
broken English replied that she did not know where
the girl had gone, but thought it likely she was with
her own people, the Ojibwas. Madge was about to
make further inquiry, when lo! through the entrance
came Pontiac himself.

One glance at that hard, painted countenance told
the startled Madge that he was in buoyant spirits.
The arrival of reinforcements must have produced
its effect upon him, and done much to quell the impatience he was beginning to feel that Detroit was
so long in falling into his hands. He spoke to his
wife, who straightway set about preparing a simple
meal for her great husband, and then turning to
Madge, who was standing near the middle of the
lodge, made her a salute which looked all the more

odd from him since it was a genuine military one. Madge replied with bright eyes and beaming smile, trying to adapt her language to that which she had heard so often from the Indian visitors at Detroit.

"The sunlight shines in the face of the great Pontiac; he is happy; and it makes the heart of Madge happy to see the chieftain thus."

"The sunlight in the face of Pontiac is that which comes from the Morning Light, the fairest among her people; if her light is withdrawn, the sky will have no sun nor moon nor stars."

This was the most overwhelming compliment she had ever heard from the dusky miscreant, and it fairly chilled her. But, after all, it was to be expected, and she must brace herself to stand a great deal more like it.

"Pontiac is a great chief; he has slain many of my people, and taken many of them prisoners; there is a prisoner in the lodge of Wa-mo-aka."

This was coming to the point quite abruptly, but Madge's soul so revolted at the flattery of the Ottawa, and she was so distressed for her friend that she could not wait as long as perhaps was prudent. The face of Pontiac darkened, and he looked steadily at her for a moment, when he walked to his couch and sat down. He motioned her to place herself beside him, but she made as if she did not understand him.

" Why does the Morning Light mourn for the white captive ? " he asked, with his black eyes still fixed upon her countenance. The girl felt the hot flush on her cheeks, but with superb poise she made answer:

" The heart of Morning Light sorrows for all her friends; she knows that Pontiac can be merciful; she begs that he will set the young man free, that he may go home to his people; surely when Pontiac's warriors are like leaves in the wood, he cares naught for any single man."

" Will it bring the sunlight back to the face of the Morning Light if Pontiac does as she wishes ? "

" Yes, O yes—my heart will be glad, and I will thank Pontiac."

He made no reply, but, seated on the buffalo robes, with her standing before him, he followed his trick of looking steadily into her countenance for some moments without speaking.

Madge's heart was throbbing painfully. Her horror was that he would attach to his promise some condition from which she would shrink as if from death. She believed he would demand that she would promise to become his squaw, and such promise she could not give to save the life that was tenfold dearer to her than her own.

It is impossible to imagine the thoughts that passed through the brain of the dusky leader during the distressing seconds that followed, and while he seemed to look her through and through. At the moment when the suspense was growing unbearable, he sprang to his feet with the exclamation:

" It shall be as Morning Light wishes ! The white prisoner shall go to his home ! "

Could she believe her senses ? Yes, there was no mistaking the words; Pontiac had given his pledge. Not only that, but he immediately strode out of the lodge, as if with the determination to do as he promised without any delay.

Madge clasped her hands and murmured: " Thank you, Pontiac ! Thank heaven ! "

He did not glance at her as he went forth, and she stood like one dazed, bewildered, and still doubting that she had heard aright.

" He said that Asher should go free; he has done it to please me. I dared not hope he would yield so quickly, but he has done so, and before the night comes Asher will be with his friends in Detroit! "

In her gratitude she clasped her hands again, and, looking upward, devoutly thanked heaven for its great mercy. Her happiness was too radiant just then for her to see all the bearings of the strange incident, or to give room for the torturing doubt that was to come to her later.

Asher Norris was seated on the robes in the tepee of Wa-mo-aka, speculating as to the outcome of the peril in which he and Madge were involved, when once more the flap of the lodge was lifted, and Pontiac stood before him, and once more the prisoner rose to his feet and made a military salute.

"Does my brother wish to go home to his people?" was his abrupt question, accompanied by his usual piercing gaze.

"It would cheer my heart to do so," replied Asher, bowing his head, but doubtful of the full meaning of the question.

He noted that for the first time the chieftain referred to him as "brother."

"It shall be as my brother wishes; let him go with Pontiac."

Facing about, the chieftain walked slowly to the opening, drew aside the flap and passed out. It need not be said that Asher Norris was not slow in following him, though he understood Indian treachery too well not to believe that it was in the mind of the chief of the Ottawas at that moment.

14

CHAPTER XXII.

FREE ?

ONE thing was clear to Asher Norris: this real or pretended release was an answer to the prayer of Madge Linwood. Pontiac would not have held out the hope to him, but for his wish to win favor in her eyes.

Be that as it may, it was not the time to hesitate or waver. On the outside of the lodge, the chieftain was awaiting him, and, without another word, he set out through the village, taking the same course as before. The prisoner could not know how much time had elapsed between Pontiac's leaving his own lodge and entering that of Wa-mo-aka, so he was unaware of the plans he had formed.

Naturally the youth looked about to see whether his previous experience was to be repeated, but he observed nothing of the warriors that had stealthily followed him to the clearing, where Pontiac met the two brother chiefs. Men, squaws, and children gazed curiously at him as he passed, but there was no interference All were too afraid of offending their ferocious leader.

Thus the journey continued until they passed beyond the village, and stood alone among the trees. Then Pontiac, who did not bring his rifle with him, once more paused and confronted his captive. As he did so, a sudden resolution took possession of Asher Norris.

"We are close to the village," he reflected, "and the Canadian settlement is between me and the river, but I shall not go back to captivity. If he undertakes to return, or to call any of his warriors to him, I will leap upon him, slay him before they can arrive, and then dash off among the trees! Whatever may be the result of this interview, it marks the end of my captivity."

He suspected and hoped that the chieftain meant to challenge him to mortal combat. He must know that Asher had learned of the presence of the four warriors within call, earlier in the day, and possibly through shamefacedness he now scorned to guard himself in the same way when the journey was repeated.

But the youth was mistaken in each instance.

"Let my brother go to Major Gladwyn and tell him that he comes from Pontiac," said that personage, folding his arms and coolly surveying him; "tell Major Gladwyn that a thousand warriors have come from the south and from the east; that a thousand more are coming from the north and west; they will soon be here; Pontiac will ask Major Gladwyn once more to surrender; if he says No, Detroit shall be burned, and not a scalp left upon the crown of any man of the garrison !"

Asher did not deem it wise at that time to reply to the boasting in similar terms.   He bowed his head and said:

" It shall be as Pontiac says, but shall I not have the company of the great Pontiac all the way ?"

" No; these shall go with him to the gate of Detroit."

As he spoke, he pointed to one side, and beyond the youth, who turned his head to read the meaning of the words, and it was with unspeakable chagrin that he saw Gray Wolf and a second warrior within a dozen paces of him.   They had come up so silently while the two were talking that the prisoner had not heard the rustling of a leaf.   It must have been that when Pontiac left the presence of Madge Linwood he lingered long enough on the way to make this arrangement with his trusted lieutenant.

It was almost a mortal disappointment, and the feelings of the youth were much like those of Pontiac, when he entered the gate of Detroit with his warriors and saw at the first glance that his plot had been betrayed, and the commandant was ready for him.   But, like that baffled miscreant, Asher repressed every sign of his mortification, and surveyed the two men as if he expected them.

Gray Wolf had tomahawk, knife, and rifle, the last the weapon belonging to the captive, while the second warrior was similarly armed. It was a hopeless fight against these two, when not a single firearm was in his grasp.

Pontiac was through with his part, and, without another word, he turned his face away and strode in the direction of his village, quickly disappearing from sight. .

The presence of Gray Wolf and his companion removed all doubt from the mind of Asher Norris as to the intended treachery on the part of Pontiac. The chieftain had resolved that the prisoner should never recross the Detroit river; he should be slain before he could make the attempt.

Everything pointed unerringly to this fact. If Pontiac meant that the young man should go free, what need of these two warriors? All that Asher could have asked was that he and the leader should part just as they had done, beyond sight of any one else. If, with such advantage, he could not take care of himself, he would absolve Pontiac from all blame.

What could be clearer than the whole plot of the Ottawa? He had promised Madge that the prisoner should be released, and would report to her

that he had led him beyond the village, and there
parted with him. This would be true, and could be
verified if she asked for it. If it should turn out
that he had failed to reach his home, the fault would
be his own in not avoiding some of the Ottawas that
were always abroad. She could not blame her royal
lover for that.

One cause of wonderment with Asher was that,
through all his perils, he had been allowed to retain
his hunting knife. He still had his powder horn
and bullet pouch, but they were of no account so
long as his rifle was in the hands of his enemy.
Either of his custodians could bring his gun to a
level and shoot him at whatever moment the whim
took possession of the savage.

Having settled into the belief that the task of
assassination was turned over to these two willing
instruments, the youth strove to think of some desperate means to defeat them. His natural thought
was of leaping upon Gray Wolf, as the more formidable of the two, wrench the gun from him,
shoot the other, and engage the former in personal
combat.

This was a wild scheme, but he would have
adopted it, had the chance offered, even with the
remote prospect of success. He reflected that the
instant he seized one of the Ottawas, the other
would take the alarm. Even if the youth's assault

was resistless, it would require a few seconds to crush Gray Wolf and place him *hors de combat*, during which his companion would not be idle.

As has been said, however, Asher Norris only needed the chance to embrace it, but Gray Wolf acted as if he held a suspicion of the determination in the brain of their captive. Both he and his companion kept several paces away, though the prisoner affected an ease that he was very far from feeling.

While events proved that Asher was right in his belief regarding these two wretches, he erred in another respect. It was fortunate for him that the opportunity did not offer for assailing Gray Wolf, for surely he never could have succeeded in his purpose. He suspected they would resume the journey to the river, passing round the upper end of the settlement, and not making any demonstration against him until the water was reached; it was this supposition that was wrong.

The two may have asked themselves the natural question as to why they should defer the pleasure of slaying one of their hereditary enemies. They knew that it was the wish of Pontiac that he should be slain, and the circumstances being such that the usual torture was out of the question, the sooner the job was over the better.

The three were probably an eighth of a mile beyond the Ottawa village and a less distance from the northern extremity of the Canadian settlement. The woods were dense, and there was a considerable undergrowth. The day was not so sultry as the preceding, the fall of rain having cooled the air, while a gentle breeze stole through the branches of the trees.

Asher glanced sharply about, but saw no one. He did not expect to discover a friend, but suspected that other warriors were threading their way to the spot. Following the motion of his eyes, the Ottawas did the same, but did not seem to be any more successful.

Asher stood looking at his guardians, but did not speak. His attitude and manner indicated that he was waiting their orders. They had started as if to lead the way, but before he began following them, they abruptly halted and talked together in low tones.

At that moment no more than a dozen yards intervened between captive and captors. The former stood motionless, intently watching them, for he saw a sinister meaning in their actions. Of what were they conversing ?

To his dismay, this had not lasted more than two minutes, when Gray Wolf emitted a peculiar exclamation, as if to attract attention, and raising the rifle in his hands, carefully sighted at Asher Norris. Although unspeakably startled, the latter darted behind the trunk of a tree near him. Since it would

have been the easiest thing in the world for the
Ottawa to shoot him while making the movement,
his refraining from doing so indicated that he
meant to have some amusement with his victim
before ending his existence. It was incompatible
with Indian nature to allow a hapless prisoner to die
a quick death when there was any chance of torturing him, even by deferring for a few minutes his
taking off. Asher had interposed the large trunk of
the oak between him and the savage, and was safe
for the moment. But he instantly risked his life
again by peeping from behind his shield to learn
what his tormentors were doing.

Gray Wolf had lowered the gun and he and his
companion were laughing so merrily that their
bodies shook—an unusual sight in an Indian. It
was high old fun for both of them.

The youth had about made up his mind to run
for it, taking his chances of dodging among the
trees, when he discovered that a change of procedure
had begun. While the second Ottawa kept his
position, Gray Wolf began moving slowly around
in a circle, with his gaze upon the tree behind
which Asher was crouching. It will be noted that
it was impossible for the trunk to screen him for
more than a few seconds. When the two Indians
stood at the corners of a triangle he would of necessity be in the range of one of them.

Gray Wolf walked slowly to the left, coming somewhat nearer so that nothing could intervene for more than a moment between him and his victim. Since to avoid him would bring Asher within sight of the other, he stood still. The tragedy might as well end then and there, providing his enemies were willing it should. As for himself, he was resolved not to furnish any more entertainment by his futile efforts to escape, when escape was out of the question.

Gray Wolf's mirth having subsided, he seemed to decide to wind up the farce at once. He raised Asher's rifle once more to a dead level and carefully sighted along the barrel. It was an appalling ordeal for the youth, thus to hold his position instead of whisking behind the tree, but he bravely did so.

Closing his eyes, he commended his soul to Him who gave it, and awaited the last awful moment.

The next moment the sharp whip-like crack of a rifle split the air, and Asher quivered as if the bullet had entered his body. But he knew the next instant that it had not.

He was unharmed! He was untouched!

"He has missed!" was the thought; "there is hope for me!"

But what meant that wild shriek which mingled with rather than followed the report of the rifle?

Dazed and at a loss as to whether he had heard

IN THE NICK OF TIME. *Page 218.*

aright, Asher stared toward the point where had stood Gray Wolf with levelled rifle. As he did so, he saw an astonishing sight.

It was the Ottawa that emitted the frenzied cry, and, at the moment Asher perceived him, he had leaped several feet into the air, with arms outstretched and the gun falling from his grasp, as he sprawled forward on his face as dead as Julius Cæsar.

" Look out, you lunkhead! there 's another of the consarned varmints!" called the invincible ranger Jo Spain from some point near at hand.

CHAPTER XXIII.

SHE 'LL DO IT.

SINCE Asher Norris stood with the tree between him and the other Ottawa, he had only to maintain his position to be safe for the moment, while by alertness he could hope to avoid any shot from him. The sound of his relative's warning told him his situation on the instant, and he did not stir.

Having discharged his Bess, the ranger could do nothing more until it was reloaded, which he set himself to do with incredible deftness, in order to give attention to the Indian that as yet was unscathed. Meanwhile he stood close to a tree, ready to dodge behind it if the warrior turned upon him.

In the thrill of the moment the youth could not help peeping cautiously from behind his shield, to see how matters stood.

The second Ottawa was dazed for an instant, and then, observing what had befallen Gray Wolf, and suspecting that other enemies were at hand, he wheeled and ran for his life. He was in the act of starting when Asher caught sight of him. Without hesitation the youth dashed from behind the tree, and with a few bounds was beside the lifeless body, and had snatched up his loaded rifle.

Events passed with a bewildering swiftness. Before he could bring the weapon to his shoulder, and ere Jo Spain could finish reloading his gun, the panic-stricken warrior had vanished among the trees in the direction of his village, when the scout strode into view, and extended his hand to his nephew.

" It looks, younker, as if I arriv at about the right time."

" Nothing could have been more providential," was the grateful response. " I had given up all hope."

" Never say die till you 're dead."

" And I was close to that! If Gray Wolf had not indulged in a little amusement you would have been too late."

" It sort of has that look; but, younker, what hev you been up to that I find you in this scrape ? What bus'ness had that varmint with your gun ? "

" It 's quite a story, Uncle Jo."

" Well, I reckon it 'll keep, and since these quarters mought become a little hot, 'spose we make a shift to a safer spot."

The ranger strode off with his long, silent tread, until they had gone several hundred yards deeper in the forest, but in a northern direction, so that they

were that much farther from the Ottawa village and
the Canadian settlement. Then, reaching a fallen
tree, he sat down on it, as if there were no such
thing in the world as hostile redmen, while Asher,
hardly able as yet to realize the wonderful fortune
that had come to him, seated himself beside him,
smiling, radiant, and happy.

" Begin, younker, and let 's hev it all."

And thus encouraged, the youth told the principal events in his experience since his arrival at
Detroit, the ranger listening attentively and now
and then making a characteristic comment.

" Things hev got sorter mixed while I was prowling through the woods," he remarked; " I knowed
nothin' 'bout Madge Linwood, till this mornin',
when Major Gladwyn told me."

" But I understood from him that you expected
to be absent for several days, so I had no thought
of receiving your help."

" It was proverdence, younker, proverdence; the
Major wanted me to take a good squar' peep at all
the Injin villages for some miles 'round, and that
was something that could n't be done under a week.
But howsumever, and inasmuch as I had n't been
out long when I seed something that I thought he
oughter know, I went back with the news. Then I
diskivered that Pontiac had several hundred varmints that had jined him from the south and it

struck me as a good thing that the Major should know that. Accordingly, as I afore obsarved, I dropped in at Detroit to tell him this mornin' when I heerd about Madge, likewise about yourself. And then I was mad."

" At whom ? "

" At you."

" And why at me ? " asked his nephew, well knowing what was coming.

" 'Cause you was such an infernal fool, and I 'spose always will be; some folks is born that way, and you 're one of them folks ! "

" What have I done that is so foolish ? "

" Do you ask me that question when you have n't forgot what 's just took place ? "

" But do you suppose, Jo, that I could remain idle at home, knowing that Madge was a prisoner of Pontiac ? "

" Did n't her own folks tell you to do the same ? "

" And mine encouraged me to do the opposite."

" That 's where you get your tomfoolery from; you inherit it. Peggy Norris, your mother, is my sister, and I have frequently made the same observation to her ever since she was a gal. In the fust place, you did n't know that Madge was in the hands of the Otterwas, but larnin' it afterwards you go nosin' round the village and got yourself took. Did you cackerlate that that was goin' to yank her out of her trouble? Did it do the same afore-said?"

There was hard sense in the rough words of the ranger, and his nephew was forced to respond after a moment's silence:

" I admit that I have acted foolishly, but, Jo, I could not sit down and mourn her as dead when I knew she was alive."

" And you thought that by goin' dead yourself it would fix things for her; howsumever, we 'll drop that part of the aforesaid subject, which I reckon the same is n't the most pleasant thing to talk about."

" You have n't told me how you happened to arrive here in the nick of time."

" There ain't much to tell. When I heerd the 'ticklers this mornin' I made a purty good guess at the truth. Madge was a prisoner at one of the villages, most likely that of Pontiac, and you was somewhere in the neighborhood tryin' to get a squint at her. So I sot out to take a peep at the nest of Otterwas over there. I was on my way to do the same, when I arriv here; that 's all there is to it."

" It is wonderful, wonderful," repeated Asher, who but for the sight of his grim relative at his side, and the presence of his good rifle in his two hands, might have fancied he was dreaming; " but," he added, rousing himself, " the dreadful fact remains that Madge is still in the power of Pontiac, and I see no way of saving her; do you ? "

Instead of directly replying, Jo Spain crossed his sinewy legs, folded his arms, so as to inclose the rifle between his knees, and stared off among the trees. He was in deep thought. Asher waited for him to speak, meantime studying the bronzed countenance, with its rugged lines, expressive of determination, mingled with a certain humorous nature which manifested itself at the most unexpected times.

He slowly shook his head.

" I don't see any way of helpin' the gal."

" Then are we to abandon her to her fate ? " demanded Asher, excitedly.

" I did n't say that, but I do say it 's 'bout the best thing for you to do, which, bein' the same aforesaid, it 's just the thing you won't do. You see the way of it is that king varmint of a Pontiac is in love with Madge."

Asher had been careful to give no intimation that such was his own conviction, and he was startled by the blunt declaration of his relative.

" Is that favorable or unfavorable ? "

" It may be either, 'cordin' to the cuteness of the gal. I consider her as cute as they make 'em."

" How will the fact that he is in love with her prove to Madge's advantage ? "

15

" Pontiac is sich a highfalutin' big-headed var-mint, like some folks I know, which the same I ain't mentionin' their names, that he 's fool 'nough to think he can git the gal to 'gree to become his squaw, and she, seein' the same can play off, keep-in' him at his distance."

" But that cannot go on forever."

" No; I sh'd ruther say not."

" Nor for very long; he will not be content to wait; he will lose patience."

" Them words of yours is true."

" The question, then, is how long can she play this double part, which must be revolting to her whole nature."

" I should say for three or four days."

" Heavens ! and what then ? "

" Don't ask me to guess; I 'll say, howsumever, that if she does n't git away from that infarnal vil-lage inside of the next three days, you 'll never see her agin."

Asher caught his breath, and yet this was the very belief that had taken possession of him. It sounded brutal, however, to hear another speak so plainly of the horrible fact.

" Is there no way you can think of by which she can be helped ? "

" It is n't clear to me now; the fust thing that naterally would come to mind is that of scoopin' in

some vallyble warrior and offerin' to trade him for
the gal, but there 's one 'bjection to that, rayther,
I should say, there 's two of the same."

" What are they ? "

"We 've got to scoop the warrior, which must be
a chief, and the way ain't clear for doin' of the
same; the next 'bjection is that bein' that Pontiac
is in love with the gal, he won't trade her off for
any dozen chiefs we might catch.   So that plan will
hev to be shelved."

" Is there no one of whom Pontiac is fond—say
his wife——"

Jo Spain interrupted his nephew with a hearty,
though silent laugh.

" Would n't the old varmint be glad to let us hev
his squaw while he kept the purty gal ? I reckon
nothin' would suit him better.   No; he don't love
any one 'ceptin' the gal aforesaid; you 've got to
think up something better than that.   Likewise,
you forgit that if he wanted to keep his reg'lar wife,
it would be as hard for us to scoop her as to pick up
Madge and run off with her."

" You hold out no hope at all! " was the despairing exclamation of Asher Norris.

" Not quite as bad as that," replied the scout,
who felt something akin to pity for his young relative, whose heart was wrapped up in the sweet girl;
" I 've been thinkin'——"

He hesitated, as if in doubt whether to express his thought.

" Tell me what it is."

" Do you know where Catharine, that Ojibwer gal, is ? "

In his hurried story, Asher had not referred to her.

" Why, she 's with Madge ! I ought to have told you."

For the first time since their meeting, the ranger showed excitement. He unfolded his arms and wheeled upon his nephew with the question:

" Are you sartain of that ? "

" I saw her; it was she who gave me the first hint of the feeling which Pontiac holds towards Madge."

The ranger refolded his arms, nodded his head several times, and said, partly to himself:

" Umph ! that begins to look better—yes, that looks better."

The heart of the youth was thrilled by hope.

" Tell me, Jo, in what way ? "

" Well, now that 's a hard thing to do, seein' as how I don't clearly see the same myself, but it 's this way: Madge is as bright as she can be, and the Ojibwer is ekerlly bright; consequently and aforesaid, when they puts their heads together, they are twice as bright as they was before; it 'll be them two agin' Pontiac, and he 'll hev to git up seventeen hours afore daybreak if he wants to outwit them critters.''

'' I hope you are right, but I have a dreadful fear.''

'' Agin', too,'' added Jo, disregarding the last remark, '' Pontiac and the rest of the varmints think the Ojibwer gal hates us folks as much as he docs. Strange that it should be so, but it 's a fact, which the same gives the gal the biggest kind of a chance to do some fine work, and, younker, she 'll do it! ''

CHAPTER XXIV.

THE PLOTTERS.

IT will be recalled that Pontiac, chief of the Ottawas, after turning over Asher Norris to the
mercies of Gray Wolf and his equally savage companion, set out to return to his village, which he
had left a short time before with the prisoner in
his charge, and to whom he had promised the freedom he never intended to grant.

The warrior who escaped the shot of Jo Spain,
the ranger, started over the same journey some time
after his chief, but reached camp at about the same
minute, because he travelled a good deal faster than
his leader.

It was a surprising story told by the messenger:
At the moment Gray Wolf held his rifle levelled to
shoot the prisoner he was killed by a party of white
men concealed in the woods near at hand, and from
whom the other Ottawa barely succeeded in escaping with his life. Asked to tell the number of
enemies, the warrior was unable to do so, but it was
his opinion that there must have been nearly or
quite a score. Gray Wolf lay where he had fallen,

unless his foes had carried away his body, something they would not be likely to do.

Pontiac did not give a thought to the one that had lost his life in trying to carry out his will. That was too common an occurrence to affect him, but he saw that in the presence of so large a party of white men near his village which caused him uneasiness. What could be their errand except to make a dash for the rescue of the white maiden who was a captive in his lodge?

He was angered that Asher Norris had succeeded after all in getting clear of his captors. He knew that the youth looked with partial eyes upon Morning Light, and he half suspected that Morning Light returned the loving looks. The only absolute surety, in a case of that nature, lay in the taking off of the youth, who, he intended, should perish as Pierre Muire, the Frenchman, had perished.

And yet, since the chieftain held Morning Light inextricably in his power, what difference could it make to him where his rival was? At any rate, it was no time now to give thought to him. The errand of the rescue party so near the village must be learned.

Pontiac, therefore, lost no time in summoning three of his most skilled scouts, whom he sent out with orders to gather the information he wished. If a dozen or twenty men were in the neighborhood, steps must be taken to ambuscade or cut them off from returning to Detroit.   Among the three war-riors was the one that would have fallen a victim to Jo Spain's rifle had he tarried but a few seconds longer until the ranger was through reloading his weapon.

Pontiac was sufficient of a philosopher to perceive how the mishap could be turned to his own account. He could now assure Morning Light that the other prisoner had not only been set free, but had gotten safely away, and would soon be at Detroit if he but exercised ordinary care.   She could not help feel-ing profoundly grateful for the immeasurable favor thus done her, and in her overflow of thankfulness would be in the right mood to appreciate the great war-chief of the Ottawas.   Would she not be proud to become the queen of him who was to be above all others of his kind ?

Because of the brief time that had passed since leaving her presence, Pontiac probably reflected that the maiden would not be quite ready to accept the statement that Asher Norris was beyond the reach of harm from his enemies.   She would wait for other proof, and it would be wiser, therefore, to remain away from her until all doubt on her part was removed.

Pontiac proved that he was not only a philoso-pher, but a sagacious lover, when he thus restrained his natural yearnings and took advantage of every incident that could be turned in his favor. He was an exception to his own people in this respect, in truth to many of the paler-faced race, for often the one with the reputation of wisdom becomes a fool when the heart is at stake.

He had halted on the edge of the village to await the return of the three scouts. His presence was noted by many, but none dared to go near him without a summons. He had smitten a warrior to the earth for speaking to him, when the chief was in one of his vicious moods.

But a light footstep caused him to turn his head, and the hard, painted face lit up when he recognized Catharine, the Ojibwa maiden, smilingly approaching. As has been intimated, Pontiac, with all his sagacity, never suspected the loyalty of this remarkable girl, who had saved the garrison of Detroit from massacre by revealing the Ottawa's plot to Major Gladwyn. He was always glad to see her, for he believed she had done him inestimable service by making known many of the secrets of the post, and he did not doubt her when she declared she would risk her life whenever he wished to do his will.

The conversation between these two will read better if liberally translated, which may thus be done.

" Ooroa," he said, addressing her by her Ojibwa name, for he never would recognize that which she had received from the white people, " Pontiac is happy to see you, for you are a true friend of your race."

" I try to be," was the hypocritical response, " but why did Pontiac allow the white captive to go back to his people ?"

" How know you that ?"

" I saw him pass with Pontiac alone, and when you came back he was not with you. I followed you, too," she added, pertly, " for I wondered what was the will of Pontiac, whose heart is too kind toward his enemies."

" It was the prayer of Morning Light, and I could not refuse her, for she is dear to Pontiac."

The pretty dark eyes of Ooroa expanded as if with wonder, when the artful girl " knew it all."

" Gray Wolf was shot and his friend ran away."

" Because there were many white men hiding in the woods."

" There was but one," said she with a scornful gesture; " he was the great hunter that they call Spain."

" Does Ooroa tell me that which her eyes told her ?"

" I do; I was hiding in the wood; I saw Gray Wolf fall, then the white man ran forward and took the hand of the prisoner that Pontiac set free; the companion of Gray Wolf forgot that he had a gun and fled to the village so fast that he almost stepped upon the heels of the great Pontiac."

Here was news for the sachem of the Ottawas. He could not doubt that Ooroa spoke the truth and that she had seen everything as described. The score of enemies had dwindled to one or rather two, since the young man secured possession of his gun and joined his friend, who went so opportunely to his help. The scouts must soon return and confirm what she had told him.

" Where goes Ooroa now ? "

" To see her friend Morning Light in the lodge of Pontiac."

" That is well, and she will tell Morning Light that the prisoner is safely on his way to the fort ? "

" That I will, indeed; she will know that Pontiac speaks with a single tongue, and shows more mercy to his enemies than they do to him."

The black eyes of the scoundrel sparkled. Who of us is not susceptible to flattery ? And the words of the Ojibwa were the most welcome that could have been uttered, for they encouraged and fanned his love for the white maiden. The wise Ooroa was playing a fine game.

" Soon," said he, with a sweeping gesture, " Pontiac will be king of all the country; there will be no white men but those he chooses may live, and they shall be the friends of Morning Light. She shall be queen over them all!"

The daubs of paint could not hide the glow of exultant anticipation which shone on his countenance at this magnificent picture. It was the dream that nerved his arm in battle, the realization of the hopes of years, an ambition whose grandeur was like that which later enabled the marvellous Corsican to overturn thrones like tenpins, to pull down and build up, until he threatened to disturb the " equilibrium of the universe."

It was at this point that the cunning Ooroa played what might be termed her trump card. Affecting to be awed by the impressiveness of the picture drawn by the great chieftain, she said:

" Let Pontiac speak to Morning Light this night, for Ooroa will talk with her and prepare her for his coming."

Strange how a man in the situation of the Ottawa sachem relies upon the frailest support! He had resolved, despite the misgivings first felt, to go into the presence of Madge Linwood and press his suit with all the ardor of his nature, which could ill brook resistance; but the counsel of one of his own race, and she belonging to the weaker sex, changed his intention on the instant.

" It shall be as Ooroa says," and without another

word, he turned his back and walked away, meeting
the scouts whom he saw returning, while the Ojibwa slowly took her way to the royal lodge.

The Ottawas who came back gave a report con-
firming what Ooroa had told the chieftain. It was
only a single white man that had come upon the
scene so unexpectedly. The trail showed that he
and the released prisoner had gone off in company,
and there was no effort to follow them, since it
would have been useless.

The messenger who first brought the startling
message seemed to expect a fierce rebuke from his
chieftain, but none was given. Pontiac may have
seen nothing blamable in the conduct of the warrior, or possibly the influence of the passion burning
in his rugged heart induced an unwonted calmness
and charity, altogether foreign to his nature.

It was now afternoon, and the sachem proceeded
to carry out a plan formed earlier in the day. He
had had a long consultation with the latest arrivals,
and it was his wish to confer with the Pottawatomies, on the western bank below Detroit. To do
so it was necessary, of course, to cross the river, and
he took with him the three scouts who had just
returned, and who had sent others to bring in the
body of Gray Wolf.

Catharine was happy because she knew that the
news she bore with her would make her friend

happy.   Her affection for Madge Linwood was
wonderfully deep and abiding.   The sweet, pure,
fragrant nature of the girl would have attracted any
one, the evil as well as the good, as was shown in
the case of the chief of the Ottawas.   It was characteristic of the love of Catharine that she was ready
to risk her life for the sake of Madge, but mingled
with and forming a part of the warp and woof of
this devotion was a vein of shrewdness and cunning
that prevented her from doing anything rash or of
a character to endanger the schemes constantly re-
volving in her mind.

That Catharine had not already imperilled her life
was because she had not seen how any good could
be accomplished by doing so.   She now felt that
the hour was at hand, and she was ready to pay the
cost.

It was fortunate for the two that Pontiac's wife
held so imperfect a knowledge of English that they
could talk with little fear of their whole meaning
being understood.   Nevertheless, the Ojibwa sat
down beside Madge and warded off the danger by
sinking her voice almost to a whisper.

" He is free! " were her first words.

Madge's eyes beamed with delight.

" No! Can it be ?   Is there no mistake ? "

And then Catharine told her story, hastening to
add:

"It was the will of Pontiac that Gray Wolf should shoot him, for, had it not been the will of Pontiac, Gray Wolf would not have dared to try to do so. He came, oh so near success, but the great hunter, Spain, was in time, and he and the one you love walked away together."

The happy Madge clasped her hands and murmured:

"Thank heaven! Asher is safe! How thankful I am!"

"But," said the Ojibwa, in a still lower whisper, and glancing furtively at the woman busy with her household duties a few feet away, "now we must think of yourself."

CHAPTER XXV.

A SURPRISE.

PONTIAC and the three Ottawa warriors walked through their own village, shortly reaching the French settlement, where their steps were as proud and indifferent as if the rude town was a subjugated one, which, in truth, was the fact, since all the inhabitants held him and his followers in the greatest possible fear. They did not glance to the right or left until they reached the edge of the river, where a number of their own canoes lay beside those used by the Canadians.

With that deference which his subjects always showed him, they waited for him to indicate which was to be used. Without speaking he pointed to a boat large enough to carry half a dozen men. They shoved it clear of the shore, and one held the prow while the chieftain stepped in and seated himself at the end which was to serve as the stern. Rather curiously, Pontiac had not his rifle with him, although each of the others was fully armed.

When he was seated the three took their places,

first laying their guns in the bottom of the craft.
They turned their backs upon him as each picked
up a paddle, so that the entire company faced in the
direction in which they were going. Bearing in
mind that the Pottawatomie village lay some distance to the south of Detroit, and on the same side
of the river, it will be noted that the most direct
course of the party was diagonally down stream.
Instead of taking that direction, however, they
headed toward the fort, a fourth of a mile below,
but in plain sight.

The Ottawa canoe was barely one hundred yards
from shore when the one at the front ceased paddling with a " huh!" which caused the other two to
stop work almost at the same instant. Pontiac had
noticed the cause of their agitation. From the
wooded shore on the other side issued another
canoe, in which were seated two persons. They
were white men, and acted as if they intended to
attack Pontiac and his companions.

The demonstration was so threatening that the
chieftain might well pause. For a few minutes no
one in the Ottawa canoe spoke, while all narrowly
studied the other boat, which continued to approach
at a deliberate speed, as if the occupants were sure
of their game and felt no need to hurry. The next
" huh!" came from Pontiac himself, and signified
that he had identified the two in the other canoe:

16

they were Jo Spain, the ranger, and his nephew, Asher Norris.

A savage chagrin must have gnawed at the heart of the sachem when he witnessed this irony of fate. The youth whom he meant treacherously to slay was now advancing to attack him!

It was the scout that was swinging his paddle in his easy fashion, while Asher, gun in hand, attentively watched the Ottawas. Although the distance was considerable, the youth was seen to bring his gun to a level and take a quick aim. Then came a blue puff of smoke, the dull report, and the bullet whistled within an inch of the head of the foremost canoeist.

It has been said more than once that Pontiac was not lacking in personal bravery. He must have bewailed that he had left his own gun behind him, but, although his companions longed to turn about and hasten to the shore they had just left, he would not permit it. Bending forward, he picked up one of the weapons from the bottom of the canoe, and aiming with the same care as the white man, let fly.

" A confounded good shot," coolly remarked the ranger, who almost felt the bullet as it spun past his temple; " now the aforesaid Mr. Joseph Spain will see whether his hand has lost its cunnin'."

He laid down his dripping paddle, picked up " Bess," and sighted her carefully at the group who

were still a goodly distance away.   Bang! and with
a single screech the foremost Ottawa leaped half to
his feet and sprawled overboard with a shock that
came within a hair of overturning the canoe.

" It sorter looks as if the aforesaid Joseph Spain
got there," remarked the scout, as he observed the
effects of his shot.

Asher had meanwhile reloaded his piece, and the
ranger was doing the same, both keeping sharp
watch of their enemies.

" If it 's all the same to you, and you haint any
'bjections to bobbin' your head, why, younker, I
beg to suggest, as aforesaid, that you bob now,
bein' as how it looks as if one of the varmints was
squintin' in this direction agin'."

But Asher Norris had not awaited the completion
of this lengthy warning, for, seeing what was coming, he crouched as low as possible in the boat.

And just then Jo Spain did a wonderful thing.
The time was insufficient for him to complete the
loading of his rifle, and, aware from what had
already taken place, that the Ottawas were adepts
in marksmanship, he snatched the gun from his
nephew's grasp, brought it to his shoulder, and fired
so quickly that it seemed impossible for him to take
any kind of aim.

His purpose was to anticipate the warrior who
was sighting with such extreme care that there was

every reason to fear the result. Had the ranger taken the same time, the report of his gun would have meant instant death for one of the Ottawas. As it was, it struck the hostile who was aiming his weapon, and, though it did not terminate his career then and there, it disabled him, and saved our friends.

The gun of the warrior was discharged, but the bullet whizzed high in the air, while the Ottawa, feeling himself " hit hard," made a spasmodic bound, much the same as his former comrade, but with so violent a wrench and twist that the canoe was overturned, and instantly the three occupants were struggling in the water.

" Younker, what do you think of that ? " asked his relative, who felt warranted in showing some pride over his skill.

" I could n't have done better myself. Twenty men like you, Uncle Jo, could clean out the whole Ottawa camp, and bring Madge home."

" Can't say as to that, but we 'd make things lively."

" What are we to do ? Try to catch any more ? "

" They 're too fur off; we 'll let 'em go."

Never had Pontiac met a more exasperating repulse than this. Had he possessed a rifle, or had not the canoe been capsized, he would have made haste to meet the two white men that had not hesitated to attack double their number. But the tables were turned with a vengeance. Hardly had the fight opened when one of the warriors was slain, a second wounded, and their canoe upset. This culmination of calamities left the Ottawas nothing to do but to get out of the scrape as best they could, and it need not be said that they lost little time in doing so.

The one first struck sank from sight, but the second swam ashore, arriving directly behind the chief and the other, who assisted him to his feet. Then they quickly passed in among the trees, for all were in dread of another shot, which was not fired, though Jo Spain indulged in a tantalizing whoop of triumph, which did not tend to soothe the feelings of the defeated hostiles.

" It 's a pity," remarked Asher, " that your first shot was not aimed at Pontiac."

·The ranger had finished reloading his gun and had taken up his paddle. He abruptly stopped while in the act of dipping it, and looked inquiringly at his nephew.

" What are you drivin' at, younker ? "

" You must have heard what I said."

" Was Pontiac in that canoe ? "

" That was he sitting in the stern, and he fired the first shot at us."

" Well, I 'll be skulped ! " exclaimed Jo, disgustedly. " Do you know, younker, that I did n't obsarve the aforesaid fact ? I had my eyes on the one in front, but since all the varmints was in a line, that don't excoos me. After this, when folks are huntin' for the biggest fool in all creation, please ask 'em to jine my name with yourn. What a pity I did n't wipe him out when I had such a chance!''

It was an extraordinary oversight on the part of the ranger, who lost on that day the opportunity of striking the most effective blow possible for Detroit, and, it must also be maintained, failed to do the Indians themselves an immeasurable service.

Pontiac showed his resolution by not returning to his village after this decisive defeat. He moved up the bank until he found a suitable canoe, into which he and his unwounded warrior entered, the chieftain taking the rifle of the wounded one, who had to limp homeward as best he could. With this boat, the leader started anew to visit the Pottawatomie village; but it is to be recorded that he kept to the eastern bank until he had reached a point opposite his destination. Even then before heading across he surveyed the river to make sure that that terrible craft and its occupants were not lying in wait for him.

This time he suffered no molestation. He received cordial welcome among his allies, but exchanged only a few words, when he noted disturbing

signs. Several months had passed since the opening of the siege, and the Pottawatomies were growing discontented. The hope of success was less
than at first, and one of the leaders intimated that
if matters did not soon improve he would withdraw.

The Ottawa brought with him the cure for this
discouragement. He had received several hundred
reinforcements within the last twenty-four hours,
besides which many more were on their way. In a
few weeks, at the furthest, there would be enough
hostiles gathered around Detroit to render its position hopeless. If it was deemed unwise to risk life
by an assault (and the American Indian generally
looks upon that style of fighting as unwise), they
could shut off all supplies and thus starve Major
Gladwyn and the garrison into submission.

Pontiac presented this view of matters with so
much force that the ardor of the Pottawatomies was
renewed, and they became eager to stay and take
part in the general jollification that would follow
the addition of Detroit to the other western posts
that had already fallen into the power of the Indians. So it was that the chieftain felt that he had
done a good and necessary work by his visit.

When Pontiac, late the same evening, entered his
lodge, it seemed to have been prepared for his coming. The night was quite cool, so that the bright
fire which illuminated the interior gave out a

warmth that was not ungrateful. The wife, as if
she divined what was coming, was absent at one of
her neighbor's, for the female members of the
aboriginal race of this country are as fond of gossip
and chat as are their civilized kindred.

There was an air of tidiness in the tepee out of
keeping with the usual appearance of such rude
dwellings. The sticks intended for the fire, as they
might be needed, were piled near it; a long bow
and quiver of arrows leaned against one of the furry
sides; the rifle of the chieftain was in another place,
with the powder horn and bullet pouch lying on
the ground near the base, while several articles of
primitive wearing apparel, partly belonging to the
chieftain and to his wife, were suspended from
the supporting saplings, which in turn supported
the buffalo robes that constituted the walls of the
dwelling.

The heart of Pontiac must have throbbed a little
more quickly when he saw the familiar form of the
maiden seated on the robes at the other side of the
tepee, with her shawl wrapped about her shoulders
and covering most of her figure. But she did not
look up as he entered. She sat with her face toward
him, but it was covered by the shawl held in position by her hands, while her wealth of luxuriant
black hair fell in masses over the face, shutting out
from view all except a small portion of the forehead.

He paused for a moment, as if uncertain of the proper course for him. Then advancing toward her, he asked in a softened voice:

" Will not Morning Light look up and greet Pontiac ?"

She did not stir or give evidence that she heard him.

" Pontiac is king of all the tribes. Soon he will be the only king in the country, and Morning Light shall be his queen! She shall be the proudest of all women!"

Unable to restrain his impatience, he stepped forward and placed his hand upon her head.

" Let Morning Light look up to Pontiac——"

At that instant the shawl and enveloping hair were flung aside, and the girl looked up, as she was besought to do.

But it was not Madge Linwood who did so, but Catharine, the Ojibwa maiden.

CHAPTER XXVI.

WHEN Catharine, the Ojibwa, ceased her conversation with Pontiac on that memorable afternoon, she knew that if her beloved friend was to be saved, it must be effected before the rise of the morrow's sun. The chieftain would not plague her with his presence until evening, but the imperial savage would accept no refusal, when he went a-wooing. She must consent to become his queen, or, in other words, his squaw. He would know that she would have learned before that time that the youth for whom she had interceded had been liberated by Pontiac, and not only that, but that he was safe beyond any further harm from the Ottawas or the other tribes in the neighborhood.

It has been told that Catharine imparted the thrilling tidings to Madge, who was overjoyed. In the midst of her rejoicing the Ojibwa reminded her that the time had come for her to think of herself.

The scheme formed by these two plotters was a simple one, being merely, as the reader has surmised, the exchange of places by the two girls, a scheme which even a century ago was not original, though this one possessed some original features.

" When it is dark you will go forth as Catharine or Ooroa, while I shall stay to meet Pontiac."

" But," protested Madge, " he will punish you, and I cannot agree that you shall suffer on my account."

There was a peculiar smile on the face of the dusky maiden, as she drew her knife from the girdle about her waist and handed it to the wondering Madge.

" Now do as I tell you. Raise the knife high, as if you meant to strike me. Tell me I must obey you or you will slay me."

Reading the meaning of the words and panto-mime, the half-amused Madge followed instructions. Then she handed the weapon back to her friend, who shook her head.

" Keep it; you may need it."

At this point in the programme, the wife of Pontiac unexpectedly entered the lodge and business was suspended for the time, but, sitting down beside each other, the two conversed in low tones and reached a full understanding.

As the afternoon wore away, the squaw stirred the fire and prepared the evening meal in her aboriginal fashion. She had brought with her a couple of plump fish, procured from some one on the outside, which were already dressed and cleaned for the coals upon which they were placed. Madge was in such a flurry over the crisis close at hand, that she had no appetite, but urged by Catharine, she forced herself to eat, for, as was said to her, there was no telling when she would gain the chance to partake of food again.

Night had no more than fairly set in when the Ojibwa took the second step in the daring plot. She told the wife of Pontiac that the chief would return before long and wished to see the two girls alone. Like an obedient and well-trained helpmate, the squaw passed out, with the certainty that she would stay away for a good while, though the possibility of her coming back and overturning everything remained to disturb the plotters.

This act on the part of Catharine was a dangerous one, for when it should come to the knowledge of the chieftain, as was certain to be the case, she would have hard work to reconcile it with her innocence. All the same, she took the risk without hesitation.

When Madge left her home some nights before in the company of Pierre Muire, her attire was such as was common with her sex on the frontier at that time. The dark brown dress was of coarse, homespun material, while the dainty feet and lower limbs were inclosed more with a view of comfort than

appearance, though none of these could conceal the
graceful contour of her figure. She wore a dark
hat, not wholly unlike those sometimes seen to-
day, except that it was devoid of all ornamentation.
This was her usual dress, but the thoughtful mother
wrapped her own plain, dull-colored shawl about
her shoulders.

" You do not need it to-night, but you may before
your return," was the explanation of the parent.

Aside from her own fair complexion, it will be
seen that this attire would identify the girl anywhere. She could not pass outside the lodge, by
day or night, without being recognized at once.
Pontiac had given the most positive orders that
while she was at liberty to leave her lodge whenever
she wished, yet she was never to be permitted to go
out of sight or beyond the bounds of the village.
To fully a dozen persons he threatened death, if
this command was disregarded, and all thus warned
knew he would keep his word. So, although it may
seem to the reader that an absurd degree of liberty
was allowed the captive, yet, in point of fact, she
was as securely guarded as was Asher Norris while
in the tepee of Wa-mo-aka.

Catharine, the Ojibwa, as has been told, was a
little older than Madge Linwood, though the difference was hardly manifest in their appearance. They
were of about the same height and each was favored

with an abundant mass of dark hair, which generally hung loose about her shoulders.

While these were the few points of resemblance, there was much variance between them. The Ojibwa had the barbaric fondness of her race for gaudy ornaments and show. From the crown of her luxuriant hair projected two stained eagle feathers, whose points, curving over, added to her striking beauty. Her chest was protected by a close-fitting jacket or deerskin, which reached to her neck and covered her arms to the wrists, the latter as well as the neck being encircled by rows of bright colored beads. Her skirt descended but a few inches below her knees, and the fringe was stained with almost as many hues as the rainbow. The leggings and moccasins were brilliantly ornamented in the same manner, so that it may be said that Catharine, the Ojibwa, was a typical Indian belle of a century ago.

Now it will be perceived that if these two girls effected a complete change of costume, their personality would undergo, to a large extent, the same transformation, provided their environments contributed to the deception. Had Madge Linwood walked out from the lodge when the sun was shining, clothed in the dress of Catharine, even to the drooping eagle feathers, she would not have gone a dozen steps before recognition, but to venture forth in the darkness of night, skilfully avoiding the glare of the fires, wherever they reached the outside, and conducting herself with discretion, she had the best of reasons for hoping for success.

And that was the plan agreed upon by the two. A complete exchange of costume was effected, Catharine insisting upon an attention to detail that seemed superfluous to her friend. When completed, the metamorphosis was striking. Even Catharine was delighted.

" Your father and mother will not know you," said the Ojibwa, her black eyes sparkling with pleasure.

" Suppose that, while I am walking through the village, a warrior speaks to me; what shall I do ? What shall I say ? "

" Do not talk with him."

" But I shall have to make some response, or he will become suspicious."

" Say that you are sad; you cannot speak."

Madge laughed.

" But it will not do to say that in English, for then he will know that something is wrong."

" Do not I speak in English ? "

" Not to an Ottawa when he addresses you in his own tongue."

Catharine saw the difficulty, and bent her head in thought. Her quick wits speedily solved the problem.

" I will teach you to say the words in Ottawa. Now listen ! "

She uttered a jumble of sounds which to Madge

had no meaning, but she quickly committed them
to memory, catching the accent and intonation with
a skill that Catharine pronounced perfect, though
the other could not help a misgiving.

" If any one addresses you that reply means that
you are sad in heart and do not wish to talk.   Now
let me hear it again.   If you should forget it hold
your peace, but you will not forget it."

Every now and then as they talked and examined
the details of their disguises, Catharine would suddenly turn upon her companion and ask her to
repeat the sentence.   Before long Madge found the
task so easy that she believed she would incur no
risk in using it with any of the Ottawas.

It having been settled as to what the course of
Madge Linwood should be, the latter now insisted
upon knowing what means her friend intended to
take to protect herself from the wrath of the terrible
Pontiac, who would not spare any one that dared
to cross his path.   Catharine made light of the
request and begged Madge to give it no thought,
but it was characteristic of the chivalrous girl that,
despite the momentous question at stake, she reso-
lutely refused to take advantage of her friend's
goodness until some assurance was received that no
harm was likely to befall her.

" You remember," said Catharine, with a peculiar smile, " that you took my knife from me, that

you raised it over your head, that you said you
would slay me unless I did as you commanded; is
not that enough ?''

'' Will Pontiac believe you ? Why did you not
cry out ?''

'' Through fear of that knife.''

'' Why did you send his wife away ?''

'' Because I knew he would wish her away when
he returned; I intended to go also when he came
back, for he would see you alone.''

Madge was still in doubt, seeing which the Ojibwa
added:

'' Have no fear. Pontiac believes Ooroa, he will
not doubt her.''

'' I will try to believe you, my dear Catharine,
but, if harm comes to you because of this, I shall
never forgive myself.''

'' The Great Spirit will protect me; let my sister
now go.''

Madge tenderly embraced and kissed her devoted
friend, who had proved her love by the dreadful risk
she had incurred for her sake alone, and then she
nerved herself for the ordeal before her.

As she drew aside the skin that served for a door
she uttered a prayer to heaven, and began conning
the words that had been taught her by the Ojibwa,
for instinctively she felt that the occasion would
soon arise for their use,

16

It was comparatively early in the evening, and dark figures were flitting here and there among the trees and tepees.   It was a proof of the close surveillance to which the Ottawas subjected the paleface captive, that the moment she appeared several warriors, one after the other, approached quite close and scrutinized her suspiciously; but her dress, dimly seen in the obscurity, and the downcast face, hardly seen at all, were sufficient, and she moved slowly onward without halt or question.

It was a curious feature of this curious proceeding that the hardest task for Madge Linwood was to restrain herself from breaking into a dash among the trees and into complete darkness.   The distance between her and perfect security was so brief that she felt as though she must change her deliberate walk into a headlong run, which in all probability would have proved fatal.

Suddenly some one struck her a sharp blow on the shoulders.   She turned like a flash, with a half-uttered expression, and saw a figure darting off in the gloom.   It was a mischievous youth, who had stolen up behind her and administered the blow in sport with the palm of his hand and then darted off before he could be recognized.   Understanding its meaning, Madge was quite content to suffer the temporary pain for the sake of the sense of additional security it brought.

On the outer verge of the tepees she came face to face with two Indians. One passed on as if he saw her not, but the second stopped directly in front of her and addressed a remark in the Ottawa tongue. Madge had the proper reply pat, and uttered it in a low tone, with downcast face; but who shall imagine her fright when she recognized the voice of the Indian as that of Pontiac ? It was the redoutable chieftain himself returning to meet her in his own lodge.

It was natural that next to Madge, he should wish to speak to the Ojibwa and learn how he stood with the fair captive. So, instead of permitting her to pass on, Pontiac stepped before her again, as she would have moved aside, and addressed another remark to her.

CHAPTER XXVII.

OUT IN THE NIGHT.

MADGE LINWOOD'S lessons in Ottawa had enabled her to master but the single expression, and it was fortunate that such was the fact, for had she branched out, assuredly she must have fallen and betrayed the secret upon whose keeping her life depended. She, therefore, did the best thing possible by repeating her remark in a feigned voice and turning aside once more as if to pass on.

Pontiac hesitated. Ooroa must have knowledge he was eager to acquire, and her declaration that she was sad and did not wish to speak only whetted his curiosity, but Ooroa was his friend, and might still be of service to him. He would not offend her. So he stood motionless, and gazed after the dim figure which quickly faded in the gloom. Then he resumed his walk toward his own lodge, never doubting that he would find Morning Light awaiting him.

Unable to resist that yearning to break into a run, Madge fled at a speed that was unsafe in the gloom, even though she had now reached a more open part of the country into which the moonlight found its way. Glancing frequently behind her, and making sure that she was not followed, she breathed more freely, and changed her pace to a walk.

Perhaps it was natural, after all, that this exceedingly narrow escape should occur. Catharine, the Ojibwa, acted upon the belief that Pontiac would not return for an hour or more, and yet he arrived at the lodge within fifteen minutes after the flight of Madge Linwood, who shuddered when she recalled by what a narrow margin she had gained her start from the royal residence.

In their discussions of the scheme the girls had neglected no contingency likely to arise. Though it would be an immeasurable gain for Madge to shake herself free of the village and its people, and though her prospects of fully eluding Pontiac were good, it remained for her to cross the river and reach Detroit before she would be really safe. Catharine cautioned her friend to keep clear of the French settlement, for, while she was liable to meet some of the Ottawas or Ojibwas, who were always there, she was equally sure of encountering treacherous white men, like Jean Chotean, who, to curry favor with Pontiac, would betray her into his hands.

The understanding was that Madge should continue up the right bank of the stream until clear of the settlement and the Indian village. When there was no doubt of that fact she was to approach the river opposite the small island lying closer to the eastern than the western shore. The problem of crossing the stream and then making her way to Detroit remained, but that was not insurmountable. If she could find no canoe nestling along the bank, she would not hesitate to swim. She was an expert, and not afraid to enter a natatorial contest against Asher Norris himself.

Catharine promised that if she could safely do so she would follow her friend and endeavor to meet her .in the neighborhood, but, unless overtaken by unexpected danger, Madge was not to wait for her.

The fugitive did not lag. Pausing only long enough to make sure that the most northern cabin of the French settlement was a considerable distance to the rear, she changed her course to the left, and, carefully picking her way through the partly wooded and partly open country, finally saw with a relief indescribable, the reflection of the moonlight on the calmly flowing river a short distance away.

She would have preferred greater darkness, for when she reached the open it seemed that a score of demon eyes were peeping from the gloom on every hand. Even the shore to which she directed her steps was without any undergrowth or trees, so that if any one were near he would assuredly observe her. It was this belief that made her extremely anxious to cross to the other side. Once there, although still in peril, she would feel that little cause for fear remained.

A devout expression escaped her when she caught sight of a canoe, drawn up the bank and directly in front of her, so that she was not forced to diverge to the right or left to reach it.

" Heaven has been kinder to me than I deserve," she murmured; " I expected no such good fortune as this."

She hurried to the little craft, and, as she expected, found nothing lacking. It was large enough to buoy two or three persons, and the paddle lay inside, as if the owner expected soon to return. Madge placed her hand on the prow to shove it clear, but at that moment some one called:

" Helloa, there! what are you doing ? "

The nerves of the girl were so highly strung that she leaped back as if from the warning of a rattle-snake, and glanced affrightedly around. The figure of a man emerged from the wood and strode toward her.

" I am sad; I do not wish to talk."

This was the expression taught to her by Catharine, the Ojibwa, but in her panic hearing herself addressed in English, she uttered the words in the same tongue.   The man who was approaching broke into hearty laughter, which continued until he stood at her side.

" Why, Catharine, there is no cause to be scared —sacre! what does this mean ? "

He had caught sight of the pale affrighted face and saw his mistake.

" It is not Catharine—it is you, Madge!   What sort of a masquerade have you started on that you have borrowed the plumes of the Ojibwa girl ? "

It was Jean Chotean who addressed her thus, and, though relieved to recognize him, Madge Linwood was not wholly freed from fear.

" Jean, I am fleeing from Pontiac.   You know I have been held a prisoner in his village.   I took Catharine's dress from her and slipped away without being noticed.   I must get across the river and back to Detroit before it is too late.   Will you not lend me your boat, that I may make haste ? "

The Frenchman shrugged his shoulders.   He had known of the girl's captivity and did not doubt that she was telling him the truth.

" This will be bad for Catharine, when Pontiac finds it out, but, my dear girl, there is no cause for haste, since the Ottawa cannot know which course you took."

" But he will search for me.   He is doing so now. His warriors will soon be here,"

" I repeat you have no cause for fear. He cannot know you are here, so why will he come here ? "

" Jean, why do you trifle with me ? Has he not a hundred warriors who come at his beck ? He will be enraged and will set them hunting for me."

" The river will soon be full of his canoes. It will not be in your power to reach the other side. It will be true wisdom for you to go home with me and stay with my wife. We will hide you, and when it is safe to do so, take you across the river."

" No, no, no! I cannot stay on this side. The only hope for me is to lose not a moment. Will you take me across ? "

" Follow my advice, Madge, and do as I say——"

The girl was standing so close to the canoe that her dress touched the prow, while Jean Chotean was several paces distant. Like a flash, Madge seized the prow and ran towards the water, shoving the craft before her. The impulse carried it a number of yards out upon the surface, she leaping into it at the instant it was leaving shore, and, while it was still going, she caught up the paddle.

The Frenchman was astounded and angered. He brought his gun to a level, exclaiming:

" I have a right to shoot a thief!"

" Shoot, if you wish! I cannot help myself!"

The weapon remained poised for a moment, but the scoundrel was not equal to the great crime. He lowered the gun with a muttered execration and watched the figure of the boat and its occupant, as it headed towards the island, not far distant. The moonlight was so clear that he could follow it with his eye, until he saw it pass around the lower end of the island, still making for the mainland. By that time, it had become so dim because of the obscurity and shadows that he could trace it no farther.

If the act of Madge Linwood needed any proof of its wisdom, it was furnished the next minute, when two Ottawa warriors emerged from the wood, in a state of excitement unusual with their race.

It proved as Madge had declared. They were already hunting for her and in such numbers, too, that some of them came to the right spot. Had she turned about to accompany Jean Chotean to his home, they would have met these very Indians before going a hundred yards, and had they arrived but a brief while sooner they must have seen her in the canoe passing around the lower end of the island.

The Frenchman displayed his treachery again, by failing to make any attempt to shield the fugitive. He said that he had come to the spot just in time to see his boat disappearing on the river. There was a woman in it, whom he supposed to be Catharine the Ojibwa, until he heard the story of the Ottawas.

Jean added what was almost the truth:

" Had I known that it was the pale face in her dress I would have slain her, at the first opportunity."

This was important news for the Ottawas, who indulged in a series of signals which demonstrated that Pontiac was using every possible means for securing the fugitive before she could reach her home. They whooped in their own peculiar way, and were immediately answered by similar calls from down-stream, showing that their signals were understood. Then they emitted the same calls, and this time the answers came from the direction of the other shore. Pontiac already had his boats on the river, if not on the other bank. This was quick work, though it was possible that those particular men were already there, when the flight of the fugitive began.

" She cannot get away! She is sure to be retaken," was the gleeful exclamation of Jean Chotean, who saw that no suspicion attached to him; " it will serve her right for stealing my boat!"

Meanwhile, Madge Linwood was conducting herself like the brave girl she was. She would have allowed the Frenchman to shoot before going to his home with him, for the story told her by Asher Norris left no room for doubt that he intended to betray her into the hands of Pontiac.

When the fellow lowered his gun, she knew there

was no call for further thought of him. As is the fashion in paddling a canoe, she faced in the direction of the craft, her bright eyes glancing in every direction, for she believed the assertion of the Frenchman that the Indians were abroad on the river as well as in the woods.

The position of the moon in the heavens threw a ribbon of shadow along the lower part of the island and the western shore. It was this protecting gloom that received and shut her from the sight of the indignant Jean Chotean, and caused him to believe she was paddling with all speed for the mainland beyond—a belief which he impressed upon the two Ottawas, and caused them to make use of it in the signalling in which they indulged.

As a result of this a canoe was observed coming up stream, soon followed by another, while almost at the same moment a third shot into sight, rounding the southern part of the island and heading toward the two warriors who from their station on land seemed to be issuing orders right and left.

" Sacre! " was the exultant exclamation of Jean.

" They must have seized her, for they are coming over the very course she took, and it was only a few minutes ago that she passed that way. They met face to face. It serves her right."

But as the boat drew near and grew more distinct, he failed to discern his own smaller craft trailing

after it. There were six brawny warriors swaying
their paddles with a vigor that showed they understood the value of time and the important crisis at
hand.

Even before the larger boat ran its prow against
the bank, it was clear that it contained no one beside the warriors themselves. Furthermore, a few
brief words made it plain that none of the same
warriors had caught a glimpse of the canoe, and the
girl who had left the same spot but a few minutes
before.

CHAPTER XXVIII.

THE CLEW.

FOR once in his life, Pontiac, chief of the Ottawas, was struck dumb with amazement.
Never dreaming of the possibility of mistake, he
placed his hand upon the head of her whom he
supposed to be Madge Linwood and asked Morning
Light, as he poetically termed her, to look up and
greet him. The girl who did so was Catharine, the
Ojibwa maiden.

The sachem leaped back, as if struck a sharp
blow. Then comprehending the trick that had been
played upon him, his soul flamed with irrestrainable
wrath. But Catharine saw the brow of thunder,
and her cunning did not desert her. Bounding to
her feet, with every appearance of terror, she said
in a tremulous voice:

" O mighty Pontiac, save me! Save me from
the pale-face woman!"

His iron fingers gripped her arm like a vise, and
in a voice of a deadly anger and hate, he said:

" Ooroa has played me false and shall die!"

It had been her intention to follow a different

course, had the arrival of the chief been delayed.
She meant to wait until Madge Linwood was safe
beyond the village and then make haste to follow
her. Why should the Ojibwa remain behind to
meet and try to placate the savage chieftain, when
she intended to stand by her friend until she was
safe within the walls of Detroit ?

She could make more than one change in her
attire, and perhaps confound herself with her seem-
ing self that had gone before, so that with a little
shrewdness she would escape unpleasant attention,
but the unexpected arrival of the sachem changed
all this. Catharine's fear was that her friend had
not gained enough start to serve her, and her act in
dropping and veiling her head was for the purpose
of securing more time for her. The trifle gained,
however, was of no account, and when she saw that
exposure must come, she remained as subtle as ever.
The part she played was that she had been terror-
ized by the white girl into obeying her, and that
she was in a state bordering on collapse, when the
chief entered, and did not recognize him until his
hand was laid upon her head.

Pontiac grasped the knife at his girdle, and half
drew it. His piercing eyes were fixed upon the girl
before him, and evidently he was asking himself:

" Is she deceiving me ? Is this real, or is it
acting ? "

And Catharine the Ojibwa stood on the very verge of death. Not only that, but she knew it, and not for an instant did her wonderful nerve desert her. She played out her part with a perfection scarcely credible. Changing her appeals for protection, as she seemed to realize that the dreadful prisoner had departed, she suddenly threw herself with the same energy upon another tack.

" Let the great Pontiac hasten! He may bring her back! Let him go quickly, or he will be too late! "

" Which way went Morning Light ? " asked the crafty chieftain, his hand still on his weapon. If she answered wrongly then he would know of a surety that she was playing him false, and he would strike her dead. If she answered rightly, then—he would doubt and wait for further proof.

" Through the door and that way," replied the Ojibwa, who, though she had not seen her friend after she passed outside the lodge, yet knew the course she followed. Catharine indicated the right direction.

Pontiac shoved his knife back in his girdle. He was not yet convinced, but he would wait a brief while.

The chieftain knew that he had met and exchanged words with the girl not many rods distant. He was ignorant of her knowledge of Ottawa, and was not surprised, therefore, by the few words she spoke. Moreover, she could not be far off, and he might yet overtake her. He hurried with all speed to the spot of meeting and some way beyond, but the eager eyes caught not the first shadowy glimpse of her. The fugitive, as the reader has learned, made too good use of her opportunity to be caught that easily.

But Pontiac lost no time. He quickly summoned a number of warriors and made known that the white captive had escaped a short time before, and that she would undoubtedly seek to cross the river as soon as possible. By his directions many hastened off to enter canoes and start out to intercept her. For himself he took another course.

Aware that Madge would devote every effort to reaching Detroit, he kept with him a dozen of his best men, the party filling two canoes, and headed almost directly for the fort at Detroit. Reaching that point with all speed, the Ottawas separated, so as to form a thin line in the woods, which completely surrounded the stockade. Through this line the fugitive would have to pass, and since the warriors, skilled in woodcraft, would hide themselves in the dense undergrowth, he believed it would be impossible for her to approach her home without discovery. What a bitter woe for her to fail when on the threshold of success!

Meantime, the other Ottawas were fully as busy as their chief. The boat that came into shore where Jean Chotean was standing, no sooner learned by what a narrow chance they had missed the fugitive than they took up the pursuit. The warriors dipped their paddles deep and sped away with utmost speed.

They had hardly started when one of the other boats arrived. In this were four Ottawas, who, being told that the girl had fled in the canoe belonging to the Frenchman, asked him to join in the search. He eagerly did so, and it is hardly to be supposed that the ardor he displayed was pretended. He knew he could be of help, and would be able instantly to identify his boat, which, being similar to many others, might be mistaken by the Indians.

When the craft containing Jean Chotean passed the lower point of the island the one that had preceded it was out of sight. The leader in the first canoe called to the other to follow him, and, pressing onward, the larger crew was found at rest under the shadow of the bank.

A short consultation was held and the course of action agreed upon. If Madge Linwood had crossed the river her canoe must be somewhere near at hand, for it was not to be supposed that in her haste she would throw away precious time by propelling her boat for any distance up- or down-stream, nor would she, after landing, pause to draw the frail craft up out of sight. It was agreed, therefore, that the two larger canoes should separate, one going up- and the other down-stream, and carefully examining the shore for the missing boat.

This plan was immediately followed. Like a couple of huge shadows the boats crept silently along the wooded bank, and drew directly away from each other. One man in each wielded the paddle, keeping as close as he could to land, while the others parted the undergrowth, carefully peer- ing and groping in the darkness. This could not be made thoroughly effective, so several landed from each boat, and kept pace with it, thus making the search so close and minute that if the missing boat was anywhere in the neighborhood discovery was inevitable.

When the two canoes were a furlong apart they paused, and the Ottawas held another council. They had not discovered the first sign of the craft in which Madge Linwood had left the eastern shore. If she had really crossed, she had landed at a higher or lower point. Had she done so ?

That was the question which occupied the thoughts of the hostiles engaged upon the remarkable hunt. Among them were some of the craftiest scouts of the Ottawa tribe, who, from the first, had been reasoning out the problem, and now began to see that another solution was probable.

By questioning the voluble Jean Chotean, those in the larger canoe learned that at the moment she passed around the southern end of the island they must have been on the river, coming from the western bank beyond, and in almost a direct line for her. If, therefore, she had kept on, she could not have escaped detection by them. But they had not so much as caught the first glimpse of her.

The conclusion was inevitable ; she had not crossed the river, but taking advantage of the band of shadows, had passed up the side of the island, and was at that moment in hiding either on the island or somewhere along its wooded banks. When this decision was made known to the others, they were surprised that it had not occurred to them before.

Inasmuch as there were two boats with which to prosecute the hunt, it could be made thorough, by their taking opposite directions and pursuing them until they met. In that way every part of the shore of the not very extensive island would pass under scrutiny and the small canoe, if hiding anywhere, was sure to be found.

The crafts parted at the lower end of the island, one going to the right and the other to the left. The former had slight expectation of finding the boat, for there was little reason to suppose the fugitive would approach that side of the island. It was not only under full glow of the moon's rays, but was behind the girl, so that, figuratively speaking, she would be following the back trail, and she was too anxious to reach home to do anything of that nature.

Jean Chotean was in the boat which, passing around the end of the island, began the cautious ascent of its eastern bank. None of the occupants followed it on shore, as was done on the mainland, for they could press the hunt without doing so. Inasmuch, also, as their task was easier than the other's, they made better progress. Thus they completed their course along the side, rounded the upper end and began descending the western rim before the other canoe had passed one half the distance.

One of the company in Jean's boat was about to step ashore when an exclamation from the second canoe arrested his action. The call meant that a discovery was made, and abandoning their own hunt, the second boat was paddled hurriedly toward its companion.

It was found a few feet from land, while the Ottawa, prowling along shore, was seen in a smaller canoe, paddle in hand, holding his newly-found craft motionless under the bow of the larger boat, of which it seemed to be a tender. All the warriors were scrutinizing the find with eager curiosity, and awaiting the arrival of the Frenchman that they might hear his verdict.

There was hardly a doubt in the minds of any one, but they awaited the settlement of the question by the only one that could speak with absolute certainty.

The new arrival was swung around to meet the smallest boat, which paddled toward it, and Jean leaned over with his hand on the gunwale and scrutinized it intently. He scarcely needed to do so, and the Ottawas were not surprised when he straightened up with the exclamation :

" That 's my canoe! That 's the one in which the pale-face girl fled ! "

Such being the fact, the corollary was established that she was on the island. She must have discovered the approach of the large boat from the western shore in time and turned into the bank of shadow to wait until it passed and gave her the opportunity to continue her flight. But that opportunity did not come. In its stead she was so hard pressed that she was forced to abandon her canoe altogether and take temporary shelter.

To Jean Chotean Madge Linwood was as good as recaptured, for how could she leave the island, now that her boat was gone, and her enemies knew where she had concealed herself ?

Still, the island, small as it was, possessed enough

extent to enable her to keep out of sight until morning. Had the Indians been double their number they could not have forced her from cover so long as the night lasted.

The leader of the Ottawas emitted a series of whoops intended to apprise all within hearing that the fox had been driven to its hole and there was no possibility of its eluding them much longer. In a short time other canoes, whose occupants interpreted the signals aright, paddled toward the island, where before midnight fully two score were gathered, awaiting the coming of morn in order to pounce down upon the hapless fugitive.

It was perhaps because of the haste with which Pontiac undertook the recapture of Madge Linwood that he failed to tell his warriors two truths which it was important they should have known, though possibly the chieftain himself was not aware of one of the truths.

CHAPTER XXIX.

THROUGH FOREST AND RIVER.

THE two truths which it was important for the searchers to know, and which Pontiac failed to tell them, were, first, that Madge Linwood, in effecting her escape, had done so in the attire of Catharine, the Ojibwa girl; and, second, that the fugitive was a swimmer of exceptional skill. It may have been that the chieftain was not aware of the latter fact, but he knew the former, and, with his well-known sagacity, he should not have forgotten to make it known to his followers, since a great deal might hinge upon it.

This ignorance prevailed among the warriors, who separated and surrounded the fort, but the remainder, who were keeping watch of the island, against whose shore the missing canoe was discovered, learned the truth from Jean Chotean, so that, as far as they were concerned, the partial disguise of the fugitive could not serve her.

From the incidents already described something has been learned of the movements of Madge which has not been directly told. It was the fact that in

passing the lower end of the island she descried the
Indian canoe just in time to avoid it. She escaped
observation because she was in shadow, while that
was in moonlight. She instantly drove her canoe
up-stream and close to shore, where, securely hidden from sight, she silently waited until the other
rounded the lower point of the island, and passed
from view in the direction of the eastern shore.

The incident warned Madge that she could not be
too careful. That was not the only canoe abroad
that night, and the signals which she heard passing
back and forth caused her much misgiving and uneasiness. Her fear was that a second canoe might
issue from the shore she was so anxious to reach,
and, meeting her in mid-stream or near the mainland, shut off all possibility of eluding it. Still, the
chances must be taken, and the longer she stayed
where she was the less likely was she to effect the
passage of the river. With this conviction, she
dipped her paddle once more, but had taken only
three strokes when she "back-pedalled" so vigorously that the canoe was forced hard against the
bank she had just left.

That which had alarmed her was another canoe,
which, like the first, would have discovered her but
for the shadow along the shore that had already
served her so well. She was now compelled to face
the problem of getting across the river in the pre-

sence of the Ottawas, who seemed to be all around
her.   Beyond question Pontiac was pressing his
hunt with vigor.

As soon as she dared, she carefully pushed her
way up the western side of the island, eager, yet
afraid, to venture out on the surface of the broad
stream.   Foot by foot she moved along, until well
toward the upper end, where she again paused, still
debating whether it would ever be possible to reach
the bank, which was " so near, and yet so far."

Finally she stepped out of the boat, and, threading her way through the wood and undergrowth,
reached the eastern side, half disposed to return to
the mainland in that direction, and ascend still farther the stream before repeating her effort to get
across.   But she saw that that was impossible.   At
the same time she did not need to be told that to
stay where she was until morning rendered discovery
certain.   She might awhile, but not for long.

While an object the size of her canoe was con-
spicuous in the moonlight, she herself would be
much less so.   A sudden inspiration came to her.

" I will swim across."

Her dress was suitable for this, and she acted
upon the resolution without delay.   Returning to
the western side, and paying no attention to her
boat, she softly entered the water and with a prayer
for deliverance, began swimming with smooth, even

stroke straight away from the spot of land that had done her so good service. She swam low in the water and avoided all haste. She was favored by the fact that the recent rain had set free a quantity of drift wood, so that she encountered limbs, and now and then trees, drifting slowly past. This made it likely that if any of the lynx-eyed Ottawas observed her, she would be taken for some of the *débris*.

Fully alive to her danger, she glanced on every side of her, and with a shiver of affright, saw one of the dreaded canoes some distance below her. Her relief was in the fact that it was heading across the river, though the fear that it was liable at any moment to turn toward her caused her to drop below the surface and swim as far as she could. When she came up, she was directly beside a large limb, floating down-stream. Grasping it with one hand, she used the other as a paddle, glad that fortune had placed so safe a shield within reach.

The trouble, however, with this was that it retarded her progress, for it was slow work to propel the float, which carried her steadily down-stream toward her enemies. Finally, she cut loose from it and again struck out for the mainland.

This time the best of fortune attended her. Although she caught shadowy glimpses of the dreaded canoes and heard the signals passing back and forth, as proof of the diligence with which the pursuit and hunt were pressed, she did not waver in her task until she passed beneath the overhanging vegetation, and, grasping a limb above her head, stepped out upon dry land.

The Detroit river had been crossed, and she believed the most difficult and dangerous part of her work was behind her. But she was mistaken.

With the same coolness and judgment displayed from the first, she went forward until a considerable distance from the shore, when she turned southward in the direction of the fort. She was now on what might be termed the home stretch. As near as she could judge she had about a mile to traverse before reaching the stockade, but did not dream of the cordon Pontiac had thrown around her city of refuge.

Fortunately the temperature of the August night was such that the bath was refreshing. Her saturated garments clung to her, but caused no discomfort. Had it been necessary it would not have been inconvenient for her to plunge into the stream again and swim to the other side.

Curious that with all the craftiness of the pursuing Ottawas, the true method of the fugitive's escape, up to this point, did not appear to occur to them, but so it was. The sagacious redmen, when they came upon the canoe, as already described, took it for granted that she was not far off, and they sat down to wait patiently for daylight, in order to trace her to her hiding-place.

This was the natural result of the forgetfulness or ignorance of one fact that it was important to know.

Madge Linwood, her heart filled with thankfulness and hope, pressed steadily through the wood toward her home. She encountered less undergrowth than on the other shore and now and then crossed small natural openings, where the space was lit up by the moon's rays. She always felt a shrinking when she came to these, and would have passed around them had it been possible, but since that could not be done, she hurried across and drew a breath of relief when among the shadows of the other side.

The only weapon she possessed was the knife, the gift of Catharine, the Ojibwa, and that would have been of slight help when she met her enemies. She had no expectation of doing so, but the fact did not lessen her caution.

According to her best judgment, she had gone about half the distance when she once more reached an open space, no more than a hundred feet in width. Its course was at right angles to the one she was pursuing. She glanced to the right and left, to learn whether she could flank the exposed tract, but could not. Not a tree was growing on it, and only a few stunted bushes appeared here and there. It suggested that a path had been cut through that portion of the wood by pioneers not long before, and the sprouting vegetation had hardly begun to refill the waste place, or it might have been that one of those tornadoes or cyclones, which appear to have been less frequent a century ago than now, had cut its swath, which nature was sluggishly seeking to hide from sight.

Madge hesitated longer than usual, until the thought that she was throwing away valuable time, spurred her to venture into the opening and to walk rapidly toward the other side. She had nearly reached it when she came face to face with an Ottawa warrior, who seemed to be awaiting her!

It was a terrifying sight when the Indian stepped foward from the bank of shadow and addressed some words to her.

Without a moment's hesitation, and with a supreme mastery of her terror, Madge put her hands to her face, bowed her head and advanced straight upon the mystified Indian.   He spoke to her again.

"My heart is sad; I cannot talk."

She uttered the words this time in pure Ottawa. She was dressed like Catharine, and the uncertain light favored her.   The warrior stood still and allowed her to pass beyond him and into the wood.

And once again was shown the result of Pontiac's

failure to notify his men of a fact which it was important for them to know.

But it was an exceedingly narrow escape, and caused Madge a shudder of fear. Her inimitable nerve had served her well, but she had learned an alarming truth: the Ottawas were between her and Detroit, and she must run the gauntlet before attaining safety.

The phase of the situation that gave her sore misgiving was that if she reached the open ground surrounding the palisades during the night time, she could not be admitted without exposing herself to imminent peril. The gate would not be opened for her until she was recognized as a friend, and that would take so long that if the Ottawas were prowling in the vicinity they would have plenty of opportunity in which to capture her. The prudent part for her seemed to be to remain concealed until morning, when she could readily open communication, bring the needed help, and escape all danger.

It was a hard task to do this. She was near home, and to remain willingly in the wood, exposed to all manner of peril, as the slow hours passed, until the light of the rising sun drove away the shadows, was a trial which it is safe to say few of her sex would have met successfully.

But Madge Linwood did it. When the bright sunlight filled the forest arches, she was a short distance to the northward of Detroit, wakeful, alert, and full of hope.

It was not the least remarkable feature of that which was remarkable throughout that these weari-some hours were passed within stone's throw of the line which Pontiac had thrown around Detroit, for no other purpose than to intercept her flight to the fort. While she sat on a fallen tree, awaiting the tedious passage of the hours, a warrior sat on a stump only a few rods away, and neither discovered nor suspected the presence of the other.

That is to say, neither did so, so long as the night.lasted. When at last darkness fled and the woods were filled with light, Madge rose from the fallen tree to resume her journey, and, as she did so, she became aware that an Ottawa was standing a little way off, rifle in hand, and intently surveying her.

It was useless to flee or to attempt to make use of her disguise. The Indian had identified her and was probably wondering at the incongruity of her dress and personality. She was in savage attire, but she was a white person.

Even in that frightful moment, Madge Linwood's courage did not forsake her. Repressing, so far as she could, her tumultuous emotion, she walked toward her enemy, and, gesticulating excitedly, said :

" Flee, Ottawa, as quick as you can! Delay not! The white hunters are about you! "

Evidently the savage understoood enough English to catch the meaning of these words, but he showed no haste in acting upon the advice. He glanced toward all the points of the compass with the quickness of a cat, and then fixed his gaze upon the girl who was now immediately before him.

" If the Ottawa waits he will be too late! He must run at once! Why does he tarry ? "

The warrior made a pretence of looking to the right and left, and then said, with a grin:

" Where white man ?—me no see him—show him —where debbil he be ? "

" He is near at hand——"

" Consarn your picter! The gal 's right! Why don't you take her advice ? "

The question was asked by Jo Spain, who walked forward from somewhere, with his rifle at full cock and his finger on the trigger. To put it mildly, the Ottawa was somewhat astonished, for he could no longer doubt the truth of the counsel just given to him.

19

CHAPTER XXX.

CONCLUSION.

THE Ottawa warrior was caught under circumstances similar to those which caused the overthrow of Gray Wolf. In this instance, however, the ranger did not shoot him, not because he was inclined to show him mercy, for the hard school in which he was trained taught him a different creed, but because he knew that the report of his gun would alarm other hostiles in the neighborhood.

Jo Spain and Asher Norris had learned of the cordon spread around Detroit, and during the night ascertained enough to know that Madge Linwood, by some means, had escaped from the Ottawa village and was striving to reach home. They set out to give the utmost aid they could, and, guided by Providence, came to the right spot at the right moment; for the welcome words of the elder were yet in his mouth when the youth also appeared on the scene. The glow on the face of Madge was no brighter than that on his when they approached and spoke to each other.

The Ottawa was one of those individuals that had

the wit to comprehend when an enemy had scored the "drop" on him, for the ranger supplemented his first greeting and threatening action by the information that if the warrior attempted to run or to emit a single yawp, he would use him as a target for a test of his marksmanship. It was sufficient to cause the Ottawa to stand motionless, glum and silent, but watchful for a chance to get away.

"Now there's no time for you two younkers to look soft and talk softer," added Jo, a piece of information altogether superfluous since the two were too sensible and too fully alive to their danger to indulge in any "spooning," "as inasmuch and aforesaid the varmints are as plenty as leaves on the ground."

"What are we to do, Jo?" asked Madge.

"Git into the fort if the thing can be done; you and the younker foller me and this sweet lookin' gentleman."

Addressing the Ottawa in his native tongue, Jo ordered him to walk in the direction of the fort.

The captive obeyed like a child, but he was as cunning as a serpent, and his captor knew it.

"The varmint means to try some trick," was the latter's thought; "I don't want to waste a bullet on him, but I'll do it if I hev to."

Before reaching the edge of the clearing which surrounded the settlement of Detroit, the party

veered to the right. The Ottawa was directly in
front, moving silently and scowlingly, with the hunter almost upon his heels and directing him as to his
course. Immediately behind the ranger came Asher
Norris and Madge Linwood, side by side, but so
impressed with the crisis that they hardly exchanged
a word or gave attention to each other.

The walk was a brief one to the margin of the
clearing. There all paused, for before them loomed
the high stockades, the bastions, and the huge gate
which distinguished the defences of the frontier
post. It was necessary now to attract the attention
of the sentinels, so that the gate would be opened
to admit the little party when they made a dash
across the open space, with the certainty of being
seen by some of the Ottawas prowling in the
vicinity.

Jo Spain gave the prisoner to understand that at
the first move on his part the youth behind him
would shoot him dead. Turning toward Asher, he
added:

" I 'm goin' to put myself in front of the varmint, so I won't be able to watch him; keep your
eye on him, younker, and if he tries to raise his
gun, let fly and don't miss, for if you do, it 's
' good-by, Uncle Jo '; but if he does anything else,
like startin' to run, don't shoot, but let him go."

" And why ? "

" He won't have 'nough time to do much harm,
and you want to save your shot."

" It shall be as you wish. Have no fear of him."

Jo was satisfied that he and his friends had not
been discovered by any of the other hostiles in the
vicinity, though such discovery was likely to occur
at any moment. He now boldly stepped forth into
view, and not only waved his hat to the sentinels
on duty, but signalled to them.

It seemed an exasperatingly hard task to attract
their attention, and while he was trying to do so,
the little group received an addition in the person of
Catharine, the Ojibwa girl, who slipped out of the
wood like a shadow, and running to the side of the
delighted Madge, placed her arm around her waist.

" I have been hunting you through most of the
night, my sister, and my heart is glad that I have
found you so near home."

" And happy and thankful am I, but O Catharine,
we are still in great peril."

Jo Spain, a few paces away, on the edge of the
wood, heard the voices and glanced back, but said
nothing, nor did he change his position or cease
swinging his cap and signalling to the stupid sentinels. The coming of Catharine disconcerted Asher
for the moment, and, though he held his rifle
pointed toward the Ottawa, he turned his head for
an instant, and smiled to note that the two girls had

changed costumes, so that unless their faces were seen, they would have been mistaken for each other.

The Ottawa prisoner took advantage like a flash of this brief diversion. With one bound he was among the trees, running like a deer. Either the ranger or the youth could have brought him down had he wished, despite the clever attempts of the fugitive to disconcert their aim, by whisking and dodging behind the trunks, but neither of them fired. Time had become so precious that the fate of the little party must be determined before this particular hostile could work them evil, and, moreover, the whites valued their ammunition too highly to throw it away.

At last the ranger caught the attention of the sentinel near the gate, who shouted across the intervening space:

" Look out for the Indians! The woods are full of them! Make a run for it! "

" Have the gate ready for us! " called back Jo Spain.

" It is ready! "

Numerous figures popped up to view on the supports behind the tops of the stockade, ready to help the fugitives in their brief run for life.

Jo looked round at his friends, as if to see that all were there.

CHECKED.

Page 294.

" The younker and I will lead, and Madge, you and Catharine follow a little way behind us; we 'll not run too fast; come on! "

They had grouped themselves together while he was speaking. No one else opened lips. They were pale but determined, for each knew that this was the final crisis. The presence of the Ojibwa with the whites settled her status, and she could no longer trust herself in the power of Pontiac or any of his followers.

The ranger wasted no time in preliminaries. He had explained his wishes and they were understood. With the last word he stepped once more into full view in the clearing, and broke into a loping run for the large gate of the stockades, Asher Norris maintaining his place at his side.

Madge waited for them to gain a slight start, when, holding the hand of her friend, she moved forward to follow them. But the Ojibwa held back and did not stir.

" Come, Catharine," said the affrighted Madge, tugging at her hand, " we must not delay a moment."

" What does my sister see ? " she asked, pointing to the right of the clearing, from which issued at that moment six or eight Ottawas, with the plain purpose of cutting off the party before they could reach the gate.

Jo Spain had been equally quick to perceive the new danger.

" Give 'em a shot, younker," he said to his companion; " it 's lucky we saved our powder."

The two stopped abruptly in their flight, brought their guns to a level and discharging them with fatal effect, both striking the Indian at whom they aimed, though it happened that they aimed at the foremost, so that one shot was thrown away. The Ottawas were checked for the moment, but others followed them from the wood and the party pressed forward again.

At this juncture the ranger discovered that neither of the girls had obeyed orders and had not yet emerged from the wood.

" What the —— is the matter with them ?" he angrily demanded, and then deliberately facing about, he called:

" Come at once, both of you!"

Having discharged their weapons, there was no time to reload. Their guns could no longer serve them, except as clubs.

But the sentinels on the stockades were not idle. Quick to note the peril of the little party, they were shooting as rapidly as they could aim and reload.

" You lead, younker," said Jo to his nephew,

who, not daring to disobey, bounded in front, while the ranger stood motionless looking toward the wood and boiling with anger that the girls did not appear.

Suddenly one of them sprang into sight, but it was not Madge. Catharine, the Ojibwa, was running with her head down, as if seeking to hide her face. But for what he had learned before, Jo Spain would have believed that she was Madge Linwood, who was still out of sight.

" What the blazes is the matter ? " demanded the ranger, puzzled by the strange scene, which was made stranger the next second by the sight of Madge herself issuing from the wood at a point a considerable distance to the left, and hurrying toward the gate that was the destination of all four.

The ranger's wishes were followed to the extent that the girls were at the rear, leaving the two men to open a way for them. This would have been impossible had not Major Gladwyn observed the extremity of the party, and, throwing open the gate, sent a score of his best men to their help.

This reinforcement ended the fight before it had fairly begun. Jo Spain and Asher Norris were standing at bay, each with his rifle clubbed, waiting to bring down the stock on the first warrior that came within reach, when there was a general stam-

pede and scattering to the wood. The charging
Ottawas had descried the others coming on a dead
run to the aid of the imperilled ones, and the sight
was more than they could stand.

But, as the hostiles reached the edge of the wood,
they turned long enough to fire at the whites. One
of the soldiers dropped dead, and Catharine, the
Ojibwa, with a faint cry, flung up her arms, fell on
her face, and lay still.

"That shot was fired by Pontiac himself!"
exclaimed the infuriated Jo Spain. "I seen him
take aim!" with an execration; and while he was
speaking the ranger snatched a gun from the fallen
soldier, and wheeled to fire at the chieftain, who
whisked out of range.

Asher Norris had run to the side of the Ojibwa
girl, over whom Madge Linwood was kneeling.
The place was too dangerous for them to remain
there, even though the hostiles had been scattered
for the time. They tenderly carried her within the
stockades, and to the home of Madge, while the
great gate was closed and barred.

Poor Catharine, the Ojibwa, was dying. The
bullet of Pontiac had sped true to its mission, and
though the grim sachem had lost the pale-face
maiden whom he hoped to make his queen, he had
his revenge in the death of the one that was the
cause of his loss.

" Good-by, sister," said Catharine, faintly, as she looked up with a sweet smile into the streaming eyes of Madge Linwood.

Madge folded her arms around the neck of her " sister," and holding her face close to her own, murmured:

" Good-by, my dear Catharine. God will reward you, for you died for me."

And it was even so. The Ojibwa had restrained Madge when the new danger broke upon them from an unexpected quarter, and sending her to another point on the margin of the clearing, deliberately ran out in advance of her, seeking to give the impression that she was the white girl, so that the Ottawas would fire at her, and thus allow time for her sister to escape. Pontiac alone penetrated the ruse, and he defeated it.

With their cheeks pressed together, with the soft hand of Madge Linwood smoothing the death damp on the brow of the stricken one, while she murmured her loving words, the spirit of Catharine, the Ojibwa, took its flight.

．　　．　　．　　．　　．　　．　　．

Pontiac's siege of Detroit is a part of history. The time came when the Indians were compelled to see the hopelessness of the giant task they had undertaken. The different tribes fell away from the great Ottawa, who, yielding to the inevitable, signed a treaty of peace and gave up the contest. A few years later, while under the influence of liquor, he was assassinated on the present site of East St. Louis by a Kaskaskia Indian, bribed thereto by an English trader.

THE END.

www.ingramcontent.com/pod-product-compliance
Lightning Source LLC
Chambersburg PA
CBHW060532030726
47498CB00004B/1165